LUNA STATION
QUARTERLY

Issue 033 | March 2018

Editor-in-Chief
Jennifer Lyn Parsons

Assistant Editors
Tara Calaby • Wanda Evans • Cathrin Hagey
Dana Mele • Megan Patton
Danielle Perry • Iona Sharma

LUNA STATION PRESS
NEW JERSEY

First Paperback Edition March 2018

ISBN: 978-1-938697-95-1

Luna Station Quarterly publishes short fiction on March 1st, June 1st,
September 1st, and December 1st. For more information and submission
guidelines, please visit our website at lunastationquarterly.com

For Luna Station Press
Creative Director - Tara Quinn Lindsey
Editor-in-Chief & Founder - Jennifer Lyn Parsons

LUNA STATION PRESS

www.lunastationpress.com

CONTENTS

Editorial

Jennifer Lyn Parsons

A software engineer by trade, Jennifer is a life-long lover of story with a capital S. Her work has been seen in various magazines and she has published three books, with quite a few more in her back pocket. She counts Jim Jarmusch and Laura Ingalls Wilder as two of her biggest influences. Make of that what you will.

When not writing either code or fiction, she reads books and comics, and sometimes makes things out of wool or paper. She finds joy in making things, be they digital or analog.

Self-care. It's starting to become a buzzword, right? It invokes images of scented candles and yoga mats and cozy nooks filled with pillows, at least if Pinterest has any say in it. People are trying to do more of it, but who knows how much thought is being put into the hows and whys of taking that time to take care of yourself. To be sure, it's about more than just taking a bubble bath, though sometimes a bubble bath will indeed get the job done.

As a side project I run a small website called selfcare.tech, which is a directory of self-care resources for those in the tech industry. (Though anyone is welcome to use them!) In creating the site a few years ago I learned more about the origins of the self care philosophy. In short, it started in the mental health profession, first recommended to patients as supportive treatment and then to practitioners themselves who work day after day in emotionally and mentally exhausting jobs. After that, activists picked up on it. Self-care became "a claiming [of] autonomy over the body as a political act against institutional, technocratic, very racist, and sexist medicine." Powerful meaning for the simple act of taking care of yourself.

The idea with self-care is that you put your own oxygen mask on first before you put it on others. Tend your own garden lest it fall to waste. The metaphors go on and on because they're needed to help people understand how important it is to take care of yourself, otherwise you will be of diminishing use to others you're trying to help and whatever work you're trying to accomplish.

So, you're probably wondering what this has to do with Luna Station Quarterly and the stories in this issue. Quite simply, reading for pleasure is an act of self-care. It takes you out of your current mindset and can put you in an entirely different one. It gives your brain something to chew on that isn't your massively long to-do list or all of the myriad problems in the world. Later on, after you've gone back to the real world, those stories you've read can filter back into your thoughts. If they've been uplifting, fun, exciting, or simply a different perspective on some hard thing you're trying to do, they can help you work in a healthier and more sustainable way to make your corner of the world a better place for yourself and those around you.

Everyone has to find their own path to self-care. I often choose meditation, keeping up with my laundry and staying organized. Those methods have worked for me, though honestly nothing gives my mind a rest as much as losing myself in a good story.

We all need each other's strength now and in the coming days as the world feels darker every day. Stories come from a well that runs deep and we can drink from it as often as need be to keep our strength up. As we kick off year nine (oh my gosh, year NINE!) of Luna Station Quarterly, I hope the stories within this issue help you find a way to your own self-care and keep your inner fires fueled up.

L S Q | 033

Notes from an Unpublished Interview with Mme. Delave, Fairy

Brittany Pladek

Brittany Pladek teaches literature in Milwaukee, Wisconsin. Her work has appeared in Lackington's and Ideomancer. She tweets, infrequently, @bpladek.

[From the records of the *New York Times*, 1937. *Archivist's note*: We have been unable to locate the piece's original author or substantiate any of its claims. We retain it nevertheless, for historical value, and because *unsubstantiated* does not mean *impossible*.]

***

Delave. It was when the Revolution failed that Faerie died, for we lost our faith in it.

[Note: In the lede, describe her: synesthetic—voice of twilight, eyes of music. Wrinkles tilted upward, as if obeying an alternate gravity.]

Bolsheviks? No, no, my dear, Jacobins: you must remember I am older than I look. There were many fairies in Louis' court, and we mostly endorsed the Revolution. That will surprise you. We love finery, it's true, but also mockery and mischief; when the Bastille fell, we thought it a fine game. Perhaps our error was that we, too, came to believe in it.

Q. Really? I had thought the fading was more recent—caused by atheism perhaps, or scientific progress.

Delave. Humans have such strange ideas about faith. You think its objects are truths, and that to lose them is to lose faith, as if you had spilled pennies.

Q. What is the proper object of faith, for a fairy?

Delave. Magic—which is to say, possibility.

[N. How she recites gnomics as if they were entries in an encyclopedia—didactic, slightly bored. My editor said: *fairies speak in figures, so you must read deeper.*]

Q. But really, the *eighteenth century?* There are human reports of entering Faerie as late as 1921.

Delave. Fantasies, alas, or hallucinations. It is gone forever.

Q. All right. Tell me about Faerie before the Revolution. Was it like Louis' court?

Delave. My dear girl. You have had dreams: you know what it was like. No, no, don't look so peevish. I will tell you, but should you interview another fairy tomorrow—you won't, will you? The tales are true, we *are* terribly vain—you shall get a different answer. Nothing is stable in Faerie; it is our greatest, perhaps our only, strength. As Europe has history, so Faerie has change. Had. [N. For just a moment, her wrinkles sag.]

Yes, in some ways Faerie was like the palace of a king, for everything there answered to desire. You see why our strength was change! Desire is mobile, which you call fickle, and see as weakness... Imagine, if you can, a Versailles of harpsong, its gables strung with doves; cities that were also woods, woods that were also water; everything ripe, potable, delicious. Fairy fruit, you called the blue apples and saffron grapes we once exported, attempting to name its particular quality of attraction: but really that quality was the land itself. For a time I lived in a watercolor town that painted itself anew every morning; for a time as a wagtail on a prince's lawn; for a time as the lawn itself. When I was at Louis' court, stepping in and out of Faerie at my leisure, I wavered gaily between marquis, mistress, chef de cuisine, palace housecat, and washerwoman. In the latter guise I held a pike at the women's march, and knit myself a liberty cap, and sang *La Marseillaise*. Oh how I sang! I remained in that form for a very long time. For years, years, I did not return to Faerie, its magic was so potent.

Q. I don't understand. How could being a poor washerwoman rival Faerie?

Delave. Darling, weren't you listening? That is what so interested us about your Revolution. It seemed for a moment as if humans had finally understood magic and endeavored to apply it to your world, the hard world, which is so difficult to change and whose possibility is, therefore, so much greater. What courage, to attempt such a spell! How could we not have been enchanted?

Q. But weren't you *hungry*?

Delave. I must apologize, my dear. I lied: there was one constant in Faerie, which was that no one was ever satisfied. Therein lay its beauty. [N. Her tone patronizing, or pitying.] Would you like a *café*?

[N. She rises, retrieves a small silver tray of coffee, meringues, and a jug of cream. Notes for atmosphere: a corner suite in the Chrysler building, diaphanously furnished, pale carpets either *haute* or threadbare. It smells of milk and cat, though there are no cats present. The rooms of a faded aristocrat: old money, old fashioned, fleeing change or the War. No evidence she is what she claims to be. Figures. Ask for a raise, a real story, and your editor sends you to interview fairies. Features, "women's interest." She looks at me, eyes *lentando*. N. for one-liner: if she is not authentic, her sadness certainly is.]

Q. When did you first notice Faerie disappearing? What was it like?

Delave. I will tell you of the first time I returned, the day the dying began. It was September beneath the Commune, and I had received suffrage, and a musket. Can you guess, my dear, which item contained more magic? No matter: what you must know is that magic is like meat, it rots, and fairies are helpless against its high reek. In the summer heat, we circled the jails like flies. That face—are you surprised, my dear? Did you think magic a child's game? I told you that Faerie answered to desire. Could such a thing be safe? Have you ever tasted fairy fruit? No questions: let me continue.

Following the fetor, I came to the Abbey de Saint-Germain-des-Prés, with many others of our kind. [N. Long pause.] When the killing began, I do not know if I participated; drunk as I was on ripe magic, I forgot much. I have forgotten so much. But suddenly waking in the heat of smoke and copper pavement, I saw that the piled bodies blocking the door were those of magic itself, bleeding its heartsblood down the cobbles. Weaving closer I realized, with horror, that I desired to sip it. I was terrified. I did not think magic could die, or that I might be an instrument in its murder. For an agonizing instant I lost sight of myself, and of Paris, for I could no longer recognize us. It was at that moment that I nipped the air and dove away, towards Faerie and her cool, sweet, possible waters.

[N. My god, is this a confession? Reminder: research the St. Germain massacre—when did the Terror begin? If it's true—! She's still talking—raving. Uncanny: everything on her sagging, dragged down. The room's grown yellow as old paper. Just afternoon light, and a crazy old woman? I thought I knew the genre of this interview, but now I'm not so sure. In the air, the milk smell's curdling.]

But death had followed me home. Not fully, not at first. But once in Faerie again, I found it harder to transform as easily as I had once done: beasts were more difficult, and flora impossible. Too, the colors had altered. Our blue apples were purpler, tending to red, the saffron grapes greener. All seemed to be growing duller, solid, like ink drying at the bottom of a well. Yet still Faerie's magic lived. Still change lingered immanent in its woods and waters, and though the blood lay still in my nostrils, I was refreshed.

I returned to Paris. It was 1793.

Q. Why did you go back?

Delave. Why, for the same reason I returned to Faerie, of course.

Q. Which was?

Delave. I believed.

[N. No, the room's definitely darker. Brown almost, like gelling oil.]

Q. When you next returned to Faerie, what was it like? How long did the fading take?

Delave. It always perplexes me that you humans call it "fading," when it was just the opposite. When I returned again, in July, the rivers had iced over, and all the milk gone to cheese. When I returned a third time, after Robespierre's fall, my tooth broke on a red apple. And when Bonaparte came, there was a hard frost. The grass turned green porcelain. The sky tinkled, hard as ice.

Faerie did not fade. It thickened to its death. Over its porous surfaces, through which passage had always been possible, crept a varnish of hard crystal. It grew opaque. Entering became difficult. Have you ever tried to run in sand, my dear? Imagine shouldering through curtains of sand, walls, when the grains are turning to glass. Ah, my sweet child, I see from your face you do not know what it is like. What luck. And what a pity, for in older days you might have passed into Faerie.

No, do not interrupt: I have nearly finished.

[N. Harder to see now. She's changed the light? Sunset breaks through the window, a red plinth.]

At last a day came—the Grande Armée was marching on Russia—when I could not enter at all. I had taken this form, my final, with effort, so that I might flee to Britain. But before I did I made one last effort. I tore at the surface of Faerie, begging its magic to ease, but my nails chipped on the slick barrier. My hand bruised against Faerie, as my heart bruised against our Republic, which had hardened into an Empire. It was gone.

Crying, I took ship with a fisherman who smuggled me and several other fairies to Dover, from thence to London, and, at last, New York. There we lived, through Austerlitz and Waterloo, though Gravelotte, through Ypres and Verdun and the Somme. All the while Faerie lay below us in its grave, blunt and dead, compressing like sandstone.

[N. It's like night in here. The macarons are slate bolts screwed to the table; furniture grows up in stalagmites. *Magic* ? I must tell my editor—incredible, if real. My breakthrough story. Progress for Women. Possibility.]

Yes: that is how I will explain it. Faerie died and buried itself, and now it is the bedrock.

Q. The bedrock? Of what, exactly?

Delave. Of everything.

[N. The room's so dark I can't see my notepad. Fight panic: concentrate. *Faeries speak in figures. Read deeper.*]

Q. You make it sound as if Faerie still exists, it's just inaccessible.

Delave. No. It is gone forever.

Q. But how can that be? You're still here—I mean, it's three o'clock, but this room is pitch black. That's magic, isn't it?

Delave. My dear, it is as I said: possibility is the only magic. And I no longer believe in it.

[N. Can't see her face, but her voice is prickly. Did I hit a nerve? Deeper.]

Q. But what about those other accounts of Faerie, even stories of human visitors? I have one from Cardiff in 1917—

Delave. All lies. My dear, I am beginning to find this interview tiring. Perhaps you should go.

[N. Air thickening now. Darkness palpable. Harder to breathe. Her voice—human?]

Q. Are you sure it isn't just you? Maybe Faerie still exists—

Delave. You should go.

Q. —but because you don't believe in it, you can't get there anymore?

Delave. Now.

Q. Isn't it—

Delave. GO.

Q. —possible—

Delave. GO.

GO.

GO.

***

HALLOWE'EN MISCHIEF A-STONE-ISHES MIDTOWN

October 31, 1937

A Hallowe'en caper for the modern age occurred on Saturday afternoon, when a swishy corner apartment in Midtown's Chrysler Building was replaced with a block of pure obsidian. The enterprising engineers of the prank remain unknown. The flat's owner, wealthy French expatriate Mme. Delave, has also gone missing, though foul play is not suspected.

A Times reporter who was at the scene has attributed the jest to fairies. She says that the petrified penthouse could be a gateway to Faerie itself. Her explanation is not widely credited.

Asked for comment, senior architect William Van Alen admits mystification as to how the mischief was achieved. "If you find those engineers, give them my card, because I want to hire them," he joked. "I have no idea how they did it. It shouldn't have been possible."

Borrowing Ark Sutherland

Meghan Cunningham

Meghan Cunningham lives in and
writes from Victoria, British Columbia.

Like a rental bike returned with a tire puncture, Ark woke up in a stranger's apartment.

He tumbled off the sofa bed and the house immediately began streaming news to his retinal slate from an extreme dog show satellite channel. Surfacing into his own brain from cognitive storage made him queasy. He staggered toward the ensuite bathroom and clutched the doorframe aggressively. The suite was mauve and dim and smelled like yesterday's fish sauce. The older man he'd woken up with allowed his irritable pink face to surface from the blankets.

When Ark felt stable he went around the room picking up his things. His back hurt between the shoulder blades. The passenger had dressed him in a sleeveless basketball jersey and cut-off jean shorts like some lo-res 90s heartthrob. American fetishist? He struggled the shorts on and muttered curses.

"You don't have to run," the older man said perfunctorily.

"What's your address?" Ark called a rideshare on his slate and checked his messages. Dilani sent him a covert warning text: *Where you at, buddy?* The notes he set to alert passengers that their twelve hours in his body were almost up were lined up near the edge of the screen, all unread. He emptied the slate and dashed off *omw* to Dilani.

The older man said, "It's six fucking AM, what are you, a commando?" Then he named an address in a part of town he wouldn't have lived in if he had an age-appropriate career. Not that Ark really had room to judge him. Then his puffy eyes narrowed. "Were you borrowing?"

"*I* wasn't," Ark said. He wondered if this was the first time this guy had been woken up by a suspiciously good-looking hookup skittering out of his dingy suite at an ungodly hour of the morning. "Kind of the point."

The guy's expression flashed from contemptuous to shifty. Ark bounced by the door waiting for the city car to answer his request. "You better not have given me anything," the guy said.

"Spare me, dude," Ark said. It was always STIs they were concerned about and not the bioethics.

The guy pursed his lips and his mouth opened with a spitty click like he wanted to say something. But Ark's slate peeped. "My car's on the way," Ark interrupted him.

"Uh, yeah, see you around," the hookup said blandly.

Ark ducked through the laundry hung up in the kitchen and opened the door onto an outdoor fourth-story landing. The sky was delicately bright. A deep-fry shack vented sick-smelling air just above the hookup's door. From the tsunami sirens the city piped a tinny recording of extinct morning birds. Beautiful sunny Port Wait-Here; built generations ago for strays from smug, gated nations on garbage in the Pacific, accumulating garbage ever since. A cluster of Superpure adherents in their shimmering ultrasilver robes drifted past the mouth of the alley, and one of them gave him a judgy look, probably sensing his aura, which he assumed was corrupt as hell.

On the street, mopeds, rickshaws and the occasional black rideshare car streamed by. Ark played 6D-mahjong in his slate until the rideshare decelerated into the spot in front of him. His heads-up noted him for good measure. *You have one co-rider,* it warned him.

He had half a mind to knock its window and wait for another car, but the person in the backseat rolled down the window a slice. Dilani raised her shaved eyebrow ridges at him. "Hey, Arkansas."

"Fuck you," he said. He slid into the car beside Dilani and knocked on the inside of the window to tell the carbot to get moving. He was a marginal member of Dilani's polycule through a girl in data nursing he hooked up with sometimes; a comfortable medium social distance to be from your trip supervisor. She shaved everywhere her body grew hair and had a sleeve tattoo of the kite festival at Colombo Pride.

"What's the view?" Dilani said. She passed him a can of guava juice from the car's minifridge and he only realized how low his fluids were when he chugged it in ten seconds; Dilani silently passed him another.

"I feel fine," Ark said. He bent over to tie his shoe. Dilani viciously yanked the jersey up his back and he yelped, "What the hell?"

"Jesus, honey," Dilani said.

Ark suddenly realized. "He did not get me a tattoo."

Dilani smirked, then looked appropriately horrified for a second, then the smirk fought back onto her face. "It's a 'Don't tread on me' flag." Before it sunk in she added, "No apostrophe."

The boss was going to fucking drown him.

***

Sufficient Aggregate operated from a respectable office above a respectable plaza and had been carefully scrubbed from every directory and signage. It wasn't even in the carbot's map; Dilani had to direct the car to the organizational alignment office in the unit below. The straight-toothed proprietor of that establishment was talking with a client in the plaza as Ark and Dilani got out of the car, and he made a huge effort not to look at them.

In the elevator, Dilani tilted her head to give Ark side-eye. "Don't try to hide it from him. Let me do the talking and I'll try to keep you out of trouble."

"No offense, Dil, but I'm going to flip if he tries to blame me for this."

"Of course he's going to blame you. You think he's going to piss off a client? Clients don't get blamed for anything."

"So let me into the ride logs! I'll go find the client. As an independent citizen."

Dilani gave him a withering look and the elevator opened. The secretary looked up with a jolt from the cam screen she was using to adjust her circle lenses. "You're back!" she said, then looked from Dilani to Ark, and her smile dimmed. "Looks like you want to see Mr. Carnation."

She pressed a button to open an entrance behind her. Only a door if you could call a featureless rectangle of blackness a door.

Even after so long working here, the sight of Carnation's office made Ark bite down on shudders. Dilani led him fearlessly into the black—she disappeared as soon as her foot went over the threshold, some cheap trick of mirrors, Ark was sure. Pretty sure.

The secretary chirped, "Good luck!" and closed the door behind them. Ark reached out to his side a few inches to make sure Dilani still existed, brushed her wrist with accidental gentleness, snapped his hand back to his side.

After a second, a zither tone went down Ark's spine, and Carnation's hologram, created by the invisible maze of lasers and mirrors in the dark call-chamber, flickered into existence in the middle of the room. Ark happened to know from experience that there was a pane of glass between them that would zap you if you, say, slammed into it on your way to approach your boss to stand up for your labor rights. There was some consensus in Ark's wing of the Aggregate that the short, handsome, graying man on the dais out there, currently adjusting a cuff on his rose-pink suit, wasn't calling in from a mansion in New Zealand at all, but had actually destroyed his body and digitized himself in the 80s to exploit an obscure tax loophole.

"Good morning, Dilani, Arkansas," he said. Ark assumed his feelings about that were made known by the analysis Carnation doubtlessly ran on their microexpressions every sixteenth of a second. "What a surprise to see you here."

"Ark, take off your shirt," Dilani said. Carnation's left brow twitched. Ark obeyed, pursing his lips, and Dilani turned him.

"Ah," Carnation said. When Ark turned back around, Carnation's expression was very smooth. "Say, that's unfortunate."

"I can get him to pay for it," Ark blurted. Dilani hissed. "Just let me into the ride log and I'll find him myself."

Carnation's right brow twitched. "We do love to see employees taking initiative," he said, with a pleasant smile. "But how about you let me deal with this one, tiger."

Ark decided to shut it.

"Lucky for you," Carnation said, "we have access to a technician in Indonesian Mindanao. I'll go ahead and schedule the appointment. The price of pork-based New Skin is actually considerably lower than the price of tattoo removal." Ark cringed. "They'll come pick you up next week. In the meantime you stay in your apartment and work on your abs, kid."

"I don't want a new *back*," Ark said.

"Well, that's what we're paying for. Now, if you get the money for a full removal procedure, I don't care where it comes from. But we don't have that in the budget. Is that *okay*, Ark?" Carnation said, with immense concern. "You can always keep the tattoo. Many of our employees in this situation just rave about their new jobs at the two-star ride clubs in the lower harbour, once they get used to the smell."

"Oh, no, your plan sounds great," Ark said. He nodded and thought about how resigned he was. Just in case Carnation had some kind of telepathy he didn't know about.

"If you win the lotto and want to change our plans, give it to the secretary. Otherwise, I'll have the boys call you. Best of luck, Arkansas. Keep on working hard."

Outside, Dilani turned to speak to him, but Ark was already headed for the stairs. "Where are you going," she said.

"Just out," Ark said. He didn't turn back so he didn't have to see her eyes narrow.

***

The client's hookup turned out to work at a do-it-yourself candy store. It was the spookied-up girl working the fry shack next door to the apartment who named his workplace; she said the hookup came in practically every day to hit on her. "He's got a citizenship on the mainland," the girl said, "so watch yourself."

The sample girl in the pink apron at the door of the shop saw Ark and decided not to offer him one of the cups of sapphire gloop on her tray, so he grabbed one to show her up and realized he didn't know what to do with it. After a second he tipped it back like a shot, which was a mistake. Spicy blue raspberry.

"Can I help—what in H are you doing here?"

Ark's face was still screwed up when he turned to see the hookup, also in a pink apron, wheeling a cart of candy boxes. He thought he'd have more time to think of something cool to say. "Can I at least get a cupcake or something?"

"No." The hookup's expression curdled. The hookup, Ark realized, thought Ark was here to flirt and was trying to figure out how to let him down gently. "Can you actually get out of my workplace?"

"This is shit," Ark said, setting the cup of spicy blue raspberry syrup on the shelf.

"Cool, I'm calling security."

"God, man, listen." He was actually in big trouble if security found him; Sufficient Aggregate probably paid off everyone up to and including 110 dispatch, and they would not be happy he was here. "Did my client get this tattoo with you? Because I'm trying to get out of here and it's going to set me back months." Lies; but hookups loved a rentee with a heart of gold trying to make it out of the life.

"Look...I don't know what to tell you. I met you—him—at 3 AM; he was stupid drunk. I didn't notice. What is it?"

"It's missing an apostrophe." Ark decided to skip over how drunk exactly his client had been when the hookup brought him home. "Did he say anything to you?"

"Uh, yeah, at some point, probably—"

"I mean *about* himself."

"Aren't you not supposed to know that?"

The samples girl monitored them suspiciously. Ark made prayer hands. "Guy, please. Just this once. I just want to ask him to help me pay for the removal. Pay it forward. Random act of kindness."

The hookup tutted and sighed. "I mean, I really don't know. I think he said he was a basketball player."

"Yeah, that was a fetish," Ark said, "so not reliable information."

"I'm thinking! I think he said he had a wife?"

"Lots of guys with wives in this city, actually."

"Oh, shit, he mentioned the Superpure," the hookup said.

Ark's heart leapt. "As in he was in it?"

"Maybe," the hookup said. "He said he was sick of Truth Committee One. It's their word for a self-crit session about how, you know, sinful and damned you are so you can be cleansed when the Martians come. Or whatever."

"Oh, fuck," Ark said. He knew exactly what Truth Committee One was. And the hookup had no idea.

"You guys good?" said sample girl.

"He's just going, Equinox," said the hookup, and gave Ark the same look as when he wanted Ark out of his apartment at 6 AM.

***

Dilani was waiting outside. Her scalp was red. "What the fuck are you doing," she said.

"Oh dear," said a customer waiting for a rideshare on the curb.

"Hey Dil, can we take this elsewhere," Ark said.

"Fuck you," Dilani said, but dragged him into an alley papered with advertisements for game jams and local cooking theater, and prodded him so hard he almost stumbled into a wet midden of food packaging. "Why were you in that shop? Did you open the case file?"

He wasn't going to lie to her. "Carnation said he doesn't care where the money comes from. Come *on*, Dil, if I take this modification, next I'm smuggling Aggregate doublecoke onto the mainland in my liver!"

"Well, you don't crack open the case file and get me in trouble," Dilani said. "What you do is transfer into trip supervision to pay off your debt like everyone else." Ark opened his mouth, but Dilani was not having it. "We have to stick by each other! What, did you think you were going to just stomp a cult leader down and get him to own up to borrowing some Portborn queer from the north side, *no* offense? He's *going* to tell Carnation, and Carnation is *going* to think I let you into the case file! I've been watching out for you, Ark!"

"I can convince him!" Ark said. "I can do it, I swear."

Dilani ran a hand over her bald head. "I've been watching out for you and when you need help you run off like some queasy client and throw me under the bus."

"That's not it," Ark said. "Dilani, look, if you want to come then come, if you're so worried I'm going to piss off the client. Is it true he's in the upper council of the Superpure?" He knew from her face it was true. "So you think he wants all his little croneys to know he spends his weekends borrowing bodies from insincere Martian sympathizers?"

Dilani said, "Blackmail never works."

"So what does work? Tell me."

"If I knew, your trip supervisor would be Jack from Hokkaido and I'd be kicking it on the mainland," Dilani snapped. She'd gotten so loud that somebody in the building above them slammed their window shut. "Ark, just take your bullshit like an adult! Sometimes you just get fucked!"

Ark kept his mouth closed as Dilani rubbed her eyelids. Finally he said, "Dil, I'm sorry, I really didn't think about what it would look like to the boss. I didn't think it could get you in trouble. You've done really good by me. If I had thought of it maybe I wouldn't have..." She nodded.

He was almost reluctant to continue and piss her off. But he wasn't going to give this up now. "I have to try this, Dil. You know that, right? Let's just go talk with him. Superpure are weird, who even knows what he'll say. Let's find him. There's only like eight people who live in the Ultimate Sphere, right? So let's find him and see. If you want to leave so bad, maybe there's enough money for you too. Right?"

Dilani kicked the flyer into the gutter half-heartedly, deflated. "Blackmail doesn't work," she said again.

"So let's stop playing games and go ask him really nicely," Ark said.

"Bit late for optimism, Arkansas." He saw her slate flicker in her pupils as she called a rideshare and his teeth gritted in anger. But when she cleared the slate, just before he could snap at her, she added, "But I'm your goddamn trip supervisor, so let's go get fucked."

***

The Ultimate Sphere floated on the Superpure private island just off the north shore. The people at the harbour let them know what suppliers were headed in that direction. Ark approached a pair of day laborers loading up crates of nata de coco into a rickety copter and told them their employer had just been arrested and the port authority was on the way, which chased them off. Then he and Dilani did the rest of the work. At dusk, they were leaning against the closed hatch in silence and Ark, finally, turned up a list of names of the members of Truth Committee One on some investigative journalism blog. "Any of these sound familiar?" he said to Dilani, transferring the link to her slate.

Dilani groaned. "I think I'd remember if I had heard one of these. He used a fake identity. Great-Enlightenment Kim. Final-Reward Hikita. Eight-Percent-Celestial Amirkhani—jack fucking pot."

"What?" Ark said, scrolling frantically.

Dilani fought laughter. "Life-Liberty-and-Happiness Lee."

Almost before she finished saying it, the pilot showed up behind her, as if from nowhere, wrapped in too many scarves. Taken off guard, Ark opened his mouth to spout his carefully concocted lie about why the laborers had transferred their contract but the pilot just said, muffled through his scarves, "We're off," and clambered into the cockpit of his death trap.

Dilani and Ark looked at each other. "I don't think he noticed we're different people," Dilani whispered. Her pupils were dilated, and she kept putting down the beginning of a grin. If anyone was born for the thrill of the heist, Ark should have guessed it'd be her.

The flight was short but terrifying. Dilani didn't try to dislodge Ark's clawed hand in the arm of her sweatshirt. The inside of the copter smelled like something burning, and the crates sloshed. Ark dared to look out over the island as they descended, while the smoky night darkened. It was barely an acre of sterile linoleum with only two features: a runway and an infrasilver geodesic dome that shimmered with other colors when light moved over it. When they landed, Ark resigned himself to death for about thirty seconds as the plane screamed down the runway before they came to a juddering stop.

Over on the mainland, lights put their fingers through the steam of the city. The air didn't smell like garbage for once, but instead it tasted like disinfectant.

A delegation of Superpure held their hoods up against the wind of the propellers. When the front representative let her hood fall back, Ark barely resisted recoiling. She'd let them replace the top of her skull with that silver metal, like some really committed conspiracy theorist's tin hat. Her smile was serene and supercilious. "We'll bring the shipment in," she said.

"The boys'll help," said the pilot. Ark looked at Dilani, who just shrugged.

Ark thought he'd have to convince them to take him to Emissary Happiness, but when he looked up and around at the warehouse-sized pantry the representatives led them into, his gaze snagged on the security camera in the corner. He stared into it. *Knock, knock.*

Sure enough, he'd barely picked up a box before a new representative, with very wide eyes, appeared in the room and led him out, muttering, "Somebody wants to see you." Dilani just raised her brows at him.

* * *

The representative escorted him down the longest hallway he'd ever been in. They were, slowly, getting closer to the featureless silver door at the end of the hall.

This is a terrible idea. The thought didn't feel bitter like pessimism would have, just weighty with objectivity, like a revelation from a god. He tried to pull up his retinal slate to message Dilani, but something in the dome prevented it from connecting; its loading animation just pulsed endlessly.

What had Dilani said? *Just take your shit like an adult?* Maybe this had been childish. His type of people didn't get to leave bad situations. They got to run on the treadmill for as long as possible and then die of exhaustion. Accepting that would have at least made the lumps easier to handle the next time. And if he failed and Carnation found out that he'd been here, he was definitely going to have to get used to the tattoo and the dead-gull smell of the lower harbour.

At the door, the representative pronounced a nonsense password confidently. The door slid open, revealing a square of silver light, the glowing negative of Carnation's office. Ark didn't think he'd ever see a room he wanted to enter less.

He squinted as they stepped through the wash of light. On the other side—an upscale parlor in all white furniture. The floor was black tile. A middle-aged guy with a clean ponytail at the base of his neck sat in an armchair. He wasn't wearing the Superpure robes but a polo shirt with a crocodile on the breast. The guy pasted on the weakest smile Ark had ever seen on a human being.

"Emissary?" the representative said uncertainly.

Emissary Happiness' forehead was unusually shiny under the lights. Ark hadn't expected to feel such a wave of hate looking at him. "Thank you for bringing him. Daughter, will you leave us by ourselves for a moment?"

The representative gave Ark an examining look before bowing out. Ark would have much preferred she stay. Lessened the odds he'd end up as #4 on that week's *Men Found Dead on Wait-Here* listicle.

"How," Happiness said, "did you get here? I thought you, your marketer said you wouldn't, I was promised complete..."

Ark wanted to wait for Happiness to get to the point on his own so he didn't interrupt the guy, but he didn't seem to be planning to stop babbling any time soon. Finally Ark had to intervene because his revulsion was clenching his throat so tight he was worried in a few seconds he wouldn't be able to talk when he tried. "Want to explain why I have a Gadsden flag tattoo?"

The humiliation on Happiness' face was so complete that Ark felt a sting of secondhand embarrassment for him. "I'm sorry," he said miserably. "It was completely...." Then, "You don't know what it's like here. Everyone constantly watching for what to do...."

"You don't know what it's like *here!*" Ark said, gesturing vaguely to himself, like to his body, or his whole life, or something. "Dude, for one thing, you can't just go borrowing people and get wasted off your shit. That's my liver."

"I never have before," Happiness said, his shrillness betraying panic. "I thought your agency would cover it!" Too rich to care much about losing his deposit, definitely too rich to care much about reading a contract.

"Turns out they aren't in the mood," Ark said. "But now that we've met, *you're* covering it. Right?"

Happiness put his hands up. "I would love to help you," he said.

"*Thank* you."

"But my accounts—I don't have any personal money, you must know that. It's all in the Pure."

Nice try. "Except for the seven thousand it ran you to borrow me, huh? That cleaned you out?"

"Committee One, we all sometimes...it helps us stay connected with the people. So we can serve you better."

"Wow, that's so nice of you."

"I can't get the money," Happiness said. "That's not how money works! It would have to wait for the next budget meeting."

"You're a fucking cult leader and you can't appropriate yourself another couple thousand dollars?"

Happiness drew himself up in a performance of anger. "This is *not* a cult, young man." Then deflated a bit.

Ark stared at him and saw him all over again. Intense pity dissolved his anger like an enzyme. Suddenly he *got* Happiness. He'd always assumed people started borrowing because they were looking for physical thrills. But Happiness looked too desperate and ashamed for that, his eyes weirdly wide. Like an animal with a broken leg, mapping out its last few hours. Happiness had hired him out because he missed freedom. Or youth, or something. He envied Ark, or the thing he thought Ark was. If Ark lashed out at him Happiness would just balk at his broken illusion. His misapprehension that Ark knew anything about freedom capped the whole mess off. Ark had sixteen dollars in his savings account right now.

Dil was right; blackmail wouldn't work. None of this guy's delusional or desperate followers cared what he'd done. But he was embarrassed and he wanted all this to go away, and he cared about feeling like a good person. Sucker.

"I know this is a long shot. But please, man, there must be somebody who can access the money," Ark said.

Happiness shook his head.

"You've *never* doled out some emergency cash," Ark said. Tried to crunch up his disbelief into a tone close-enough to desperation.

Now Happiness hesitated. He was wearing down. "Only to

the neighbourhood churches," he said finally, reluctantly. "And people on their membership rolls."

Ark suddenly got a feeling. Not a good feeling or a bad feeling. If anything a feeling that said with reservation, *well, here we go.* "So if I joined the Superpure, you would say..."

Happiness just said, very weakly, "Hmm."

***

Ark and Dilani didn't make it back to the mainland until around 3 AM, when Dilani learned that the rideshare grid to her neighbourhood was browned out. "Come crash at my place," Ark said. They were both tired enough to flop onto the same mattress together. When Ark woke up with Dilani drooling on his chest he decided, though with affection, that this whole trauma bonding thing was a bit overrated.

There were two messages waiting for him in the slate as he cracked open a window to smoke out of it—the kind of perfunctory window installed to halfheartedly satisfy zoning requirements, only just big enough for his arm and the joint. Outside, dead birds sang and a busker played experimental zither on a street corner to claps and occasional jeers.

The first message came wrapped in infrasilver, which made his eyes hurt. *Lester,* the message started. Ark tsked at the sight of his legal name; a benefit of a country with bad record-keeping was that it was easy to leave a name like Lester behind. He was already thinking of finding something new. The whole American theme was going sour.

I have requested that the financial department of your neighbourhood church immediately forward the full cost of a laser-based tattoo removal procedure to the Sufficient Aggregate under the guise of a charitable donation from your long-time spiritual community.

Awesome, but Ark already knew the catch was coming.

In order to do so I have personally enrolled you as an honorary member of your Superpure chapter at the Seeking Enlightenment rewards tier. You will have to attend twenty hours of community service a month to maintain your membership...

There it was.

...but you will also receive a monthly allowance of three hundred dollars from upper leadership. I hope this is sufficient incentive for you to remain an active member of our movement and see what we can offer you. I sincerely hope you find some kind of peace through this opportunity. When I was a young man, and Ark stopped reading.

He didn't get to enjoy the thought of an extra three hundred dollars for even a second, because the second letter was from the Aggregate. And it was stamped with an encryption signature Ark hadn't seen before. A bright pink one. Ark exhaled smoke and ran his tongue over his teeth, avoiding it.

Dilani groaned as she rolled from the bed. "Where's your bathroom?" she said.

"Only other door," Ark said. "Hey," he said after another second, and she paused in the middle of grinding sleep grit out of her eye. "Do you want three hundred dollars a month?"

"What?" she said.

He was embarrassed. "I get it through the Superpure. I'm doing fine right now, I'll save up a cushion for the first few months. But

I don't need the rest. You want to buy tickets to the mainland, right? Go to some tech-support college in Bolivia or whatever?"

"Ark," she said. "I couldn't...that's a lot of money."

"Well, if you don't want to accept a gift you can also do my community service," Ark said, and sucked his joint like a long-suffering soldier.

"They want *you* to do..." Dilani said, then started laughing, and laughed all the way to the bathroom door.

Ark had no excuses left, and anyways, his anxiety was going down a little bit. He opened the second message.

The letterhead contained a classy graphic of a carnation that slowly bloomed and unbloomed. The message wasn't signed. It just said: *Strike two, kid. But when you hit strike three, there are places in corporate for salespeople who know how to take initiative.*

Ark snorted, rolled his eyes, deleted them both. Out on the sidewalk, the zither man finished his cover of ...*Baby One More Time* and the crowd clapped. Ark set down the joint so he could clap too. Apparently it was loud enough that the zither man looked over his shoulder and, with a rotting and genuine smile, threw up a peace sign toward Ark's window.

The Palm Bride

Diana Hurlburt

Diana Hurlburt is a librarian and writer
in Florida. Selections of her short fiction
can be found at Kaaterskill Basin, Body
Parts, cahoodaloodaling, and The
Hanging Garden, and in the anthologies
Beyond the Pillars and Equus. Her
debut novella is forthcoming from
Riptide in 2018.

Some said, disapproving, that more accurately she was the *Palmer's* Bride, the dolly created by lonely pilgrims en route to the flowering coast—holy men, so called, who after all were only mortal, carnal. Others swore she was a native custom, an idol created to be destroyed, a dummy of fronds and bark named and then submerged in a blue hole. Whatever the root—import or homegrown, Christian or pagan or likeliest of all the unremarkable marriage of both—the Palm Bride grew and waned every year. She was born on the last sliver of the November moon. She died, or occasionally lived, on the full moon closest to Christmas. She brought favor, or plague. She was ephemeral, the mark of her footfalls palpable, permanent.

Any man could seek her.

***

Annabel Randolph arrived at Villa Reina with little ceremony and even less warning.

She halted in a cloud of pale dust and looked through gates green with verdigris and tangled trumpet vine. The Huguenot cemetery lay south, and a fine grove of oranges northeast, and the crooked neck of the St. Sebastian due north, and in this triangle—a holy symbol, Miss Randolph thought—perched the Villa: a grand duchess of a house, cloistered as a nun among its pines. A red-tiled roof rose above trees in the distance. The gates were locked.

"Mrs. Cobb," Miss Randolph repeated to the sullen-eyed man who had sauntered out of a path through the Spanish bayonets as though he had nothing better to do than stare and parrot simple requests.

He scratched at a forelock of whitish-blond hair. "Miss Butler is the lady of the house."

"Nonetheless," Miss Randolph said, secure in the superiority of her knowledge. "I would like to speak with Mrs. Cobb."

The man disappeared, leaving Miss Randolph alone with the beaming sun. She wanted to remove her hat, perhaps loosen her collar, but refused to meet Jessamine Cobb in such a state. Extracting a fan from her carpet bag, she snapped it open and drove it through a hovering cloud of mosquitoes. Despite the late-November calendar date, both insect and floral life abounded. The flowering coast indeed, as though Florida was not pure swamp and wilds... as though even its most historic city had anything to compare to the cultivation and cosmopolitan niceties of New York. It was just like them, Miss Randolph thought, *them* being the addle-pated settlers who'd stumbled south and never had the sense to flee back past the Mason-Dixon Line upon encountering alligators and malaria, so very like them to have roused a spirit such as this—to have opened a gateway with such a resounding echo that it was audible all the way up to Seneca Falls.

She waited, waving her fan and slapping flies, unwinding a tendril of vine from where it wrapped around her shoulder. It retreated reluctantly, leaving behind a spattering of bright pollen on her sleeve.

The man returned, and the gates to Villa Reina opened.

The sitting room, at least, did not strike Miss Randolph as haunted. She perched on the settee and arranged her skirts and looked calmly at Mrs. Jessamine Cobb. There was another woman in the room as well, but Miss Randolph's attention remained on Mrs. Cobb: her gown of cornflower blue, modest in style but well-made, and the turban which hid her hair; her broad, high forehead and fine black eyebrows; the slight shape of her beneath gown and petticoats all contributing to a luminous delicacy composed of burnished brown skin and sharp wrist bones and long, smiling lips.

"Mrs. Randolph," Mrs. Cobb said, faintly questioning. "Welcome to St. Augustine."

"Miss," Miss Randolph said. "I have never married. The company of men is pleasant in some arenas of life, but ultimately unnecessary. St. Augustine seems a fine city."

City was generous.

"We've many diversions," Mrs. Cobb said. "Forgive my confusion. Not being much traveled, I'm unsure of some prior meeting, in time or locale."

She spoke precisely, her voice a pleasant alto and accented with the Carolinas. Her former master, as Miss Randolph had heard it told, had originated in Charleston and moved down the coast after her husband's death, freeing slaves as she went, until she landed at last in the nation's oldest settlement. Either love or a wish to make reparations placed the Villa in Mrs. Cobb's control after the woman's death, though Miss Randolph knew appearances must be kept. Presumably that was why the man at the gate believed the second woman in this room, who was white, to be the house's owner.

Miss Randolph doubted that a house such as this could truly have an owner. Though its trappings were still fine, the longer she sat in her chair, the more discomfited she became. The sun outside was too bright, the air within too close, the women too calm for a spiritual disturbance of this magnitude. She had seen the looted remnants of finer houses on her journey south, yet Villa Reina remained.

"If we have met," Miss Randolph said, "it would be in that space which is outside time and locale." She folded her hands in their black lacy mitts and watched Mrs. Cobb for signs of trouble. "I wonder how it is that you manage to fool those so nearby, yet your doings are known to us as far away as New York. You have a mighty voice, Mrs. Cobb."

"I can't think what you mean," Mrs. Cobb said. The blue of her gown matched that of the embroidery on her chair, and that of the chair opposite the fireplace, upon which the other woman sat. Miss Randolph appreciated a flair for scene-setting. Mrs. Cobb continued, "A sense of discretion is necessary. You understand, Miss Randolph. We're not all so blessed with an abundance of—movements." She smiled, the expression's politeness belied by dark, intense eyes. "Theosophy, suffrage, all these conventions you hold in New York and the capital. What is it like, such openness? How we might have caught your attention so far south, with our backwoods ways..."

A flash of steel, then, beneath the velvet.

The woman opposite Mrs. Cobb rearranged her skirts in a rustle of crinolines. She was dressed more richly, a gown of fashionable magenta doing her faded ginger hair and pale complexion no favors. She struck Miss Randolph as wind-worn, eroded by salt air, round and featureless as the sand dunes to the east. Still she said nothing.

"When a spirit as powerful as this is called down, the effects are felt throughout the movement," Miss Randolph said. *Go to them,* one of her fellows had said urgently, after a session in which certain writings revealed the rough shape of the spirit's terrain. "I wondered if I might be of some service."

The white woman's eyes caught Mrs. Cobb's eloquently indeed. Miss Randolph sat up a little straighter on the settee. Was it possible the two were not aware?

"I don't know that we can afford to reimburse your train ticket," Mrs. Cobb said, laughing. "Our small press doesn't bring much money, only a bit of notoriety. My companion—" Miss Randolph restrained her own laughter. "Miss Butler, of whom you've surely heard, is frugal, but the estate takes upkeep. Miss Randolph, forgive me, but I'm not sure this small matter was worth your trip."

A polite way of wishing someone back from whence they'd come.

"The strength of this spirit is no small matter," Miss Randolph returned. "Why, the evening of its arrival—"

"She has a name," said Mrs. Cobb.

She. Miss Randolph considered. The spirit in question had struck her only with its strength—her, sweating in the night, and a few others of the Seneca Falls group woken similarly, shaken and drained. "It does not seem to me the type of spirit to retain personality," she said. "Thought, feeling... I received no notion that it might be a guide, or an emissary."

"Perhaps it's only that you don't know her," Mrs. Cobb said. She raised a hand, her palm indicating the large window to the north, through which were visible a pine grove and a white, chalky path. "Would you like to meet her?"

**

Miss Randolph surveyed the pitiful brown bundle placed too carefully for its elements at the base of a knotty pine.

"The Palm Bride," Mrs. Cobb said. Her voice did not carry within the thicket, and the air was cool among the trees, little sun piercing their canopy. "It's unusual for her effects to be so pronounced."

"What has this—" Miss Randolph flapped her fan at the fronds and bark beneath the pine. "This *manikin*, you say it's something to do with the spirit? How so? Spirits are manifested through proper formation of séance, or perhaps, if they are not strong, through photographic plates or writings. I have never seen nor heard of such crude—"

"There are more things in Heaven and Earth," Miss Butler said, and Miss Randolph did not consider this quotation an improvement on the woman's earlier silence.

"A prop, then," she said. "I've seen mediums who use such items. A doll belonging to the departed spirit, or a portrait. There must be some connection with the spirit for the item to conduct with efficacy. And this?" She waved her fan again. The heap of brush took no offense. "What possible connection could bark and palm fronds have to this spirit?"

"We aren't concerned with the sympathy of magic, in this case." Mrs. Cobb's face remained serene. Neither she nor Miss Butler had touched the dead matter, and Miss Randolph decided that in this, at least, they knew best. "The Palm Bride is a case of—how would you phrase it, Mae?"

"Embodiment," Miss Butler said. Her voice was low, a drone barely distinguishable in tempo from the mosquitoes whining near Miss Randolph's ear, and carrying a hint of Boston, like the rind of a good cheese. Her expression was detached, neither calm as Mrs. Cobb's nor avid as Miss Randolph knew her own must be. "It's a vessel, no more. Any man might create a Palm Bride, but he can't expect it to perform. It's not a puppet. It's made of dreams."

"Superstition," Miss Randolph said, and startled as a low-hanging pine branch brushed her back with light fingers. "A folk belief, no doubt. It's miraculous men hold to such shaky reasoning, in this age."

"Many men did not return from the war," Mrs. Cobb said. "Many more did, and wished they hadn't. They came home to women raped and land stolen, farms burned. They left on the assurance of freedom and returned to a new sort of bondage." A hand, long and elegant, adjusted the base of her turban. "Men's natures are the seeking sort."

"Women," Miss Butler supplied, as though Miss Randolph could not be given to assume what men might seek. "Often they believe the Bride brings them a wife."

Miss Randolph considered the manifold follies of men, and all the things one might seek prior to building a wife out of kindling and underbrush. She didn't like the Bride. Now that she had seen it, and dismissed it for litter and refuse, it seemed that a face flickered in its fronds—something slippery and vanishing, a rustle and a wink. The thin sunlight entering the pines illuminated the Bride, as though the hand of deity drew attention to it.

49

"If it is a man's tradition, why is it here in your grove, Mrs. Cobb?"

A faint expression of disgust crossed Miss Butler's face. "Why, neither of us built it, if that's your insinuation. It's meant for fun. A silly tradition for boys. No harm ever came of it that I heard."

"She's always been here." Mrs. Cobb touched the pine's trunk, and then pointed to a stump some feet away, her index finger drawing a line between the living tree and the dead. "She may be a spirit now, and a bit livelier than most, but there was a time in which she was a goddess."

"You don't know that," Miss Butler said, her voice dipping lower in an aside Miss Randolph suspected she was not meant to hear.

"Her face seems one way to me, and another to Miss Butler," Mrs. Cobb said, still smiling. "Both being transplants to this coast, neither of us can quite claim her. We differ somewhat in the particulars."

"You may be as particular as you please," Miss Randolph said, and she turned from the fronds beneath the pine. The sight of the heap—a *Bride*, and who would call it such?—was beginning to turn her stomach, which never traveled well to begin with. "My concern is in banishing it."

***

"We don't often use the dining room," Mrs. Cobb said.

"Not for dining, at any rate," Miss Butler added.

"One space is as good as another," Miss Randolph said. She gazed at the room's lavish bookshelves, its broad cherry-wood table and velveteen chair cushions. She supposed once upon a time it had hosted the finest of coastal society; now its opulence was muted, turned utilitarian and bookish. It was fortunate the room, and the rest of Villa Reina, had not fallen to pillaging or ruin as Confederate troops stumbled home and hordes of Miss Randolph's own opportunistic countrymen poured south. *Fortune,* she thought, *or something stronger.* She said, "Before we make our preparations, may I compile some notes?"

"Our home is yours, Miss Randolph," Mrs. Cobb said. "Mae, perhaps some tea?"

"Tea would be most welcome," Miss Randolph said, settling her traveling satchel in her lap.

She had no desire to admit weakness, but the train trip from Rochester to Fernandina Beach had wearied her, and the carriage ride to St. Augustine had been more tiring still. It troubled her a bit, how pleasant the air felt here, and how quickly the lingering chill of Seneca Falls had been driven from her bones.

She decided no remarks were necessary on the arrangement of Miss Butler busying herself with the tea service, and Mrs. Cobb sitting at the table's head with hands folded.

"Now." Miss Randolph removed a small leather-bound book from her satchel and inhaled appreciatively as scents of orange and clove filled the air. "The spirit first rose on the night of November twenty-second, is that correct?"

"In its essentials."

Miss Randolph's pencil paused. "Is it correct or is it not? I value accuracy, for the sake of our record-keeping."

"As you measure such things," said Mrs. Cobb, "that's correct."

"Jessamine." Miss Butler set the tea service down on the table with a loud clunk. "Miss Randolph. If you'll excuse us. You've stumbled into a long-ranging discussion." Her tone remained flat, but Miss Randolph detected a note of dismissal, the suggestion that she was not welcome in the aforementioned discussion. "November twenty-second marks the Bride's birth, and no bones about it."

"Birth," Miss Randolph noted, pencil scratching busily. "A curious term. The more usual wording is *manifestation,* but..." She jotted a few notes, pondering. "So it has been loose for nearly a week, then. And you had no thought of banishing it?"

Her intent had not been to pass judgment. That was merely the timbre of her voice.

Miss Butler's hand remained steady as she filled Miss Randolph's cup. She made no comment. Mrs. Cobb sipped her tea. The china was fine, a white so lucid it was nearly transparent, the tea within dark and rich.

"We wished to find out who called her," Mrs. Cobb said. "Before any attempts were made."

It was sensible enough. Miss Randolph hoped such basic questions had been answered. "And did you?"

"His name is Wyn Bradley," Mrs. Cobb said. "You met him. He keeps the grounds here, and completes jobs—the firewood, clearing brush, tending the horse."

"A veteran," Miss Butler said brusquely. "His gray coat had lost its dye by the time he came home, but all soldiers have a look about them."

The man at the Villa's gates had had a look, certainly, Miss Randolph reflected. Some shadow of starvation, though he was well-fed once more, and a residue of blood, though he looked to have washed recently. The spiritual stains of warfare were not so easily removed. It wore on her, the presence of the men returning to Seneca Falls: the hollows carved into familiar faces, the irrevocable changes violence wrought, the death that clung to them regardless of baths or new clothing.

So many more women now, crying for séances to reach forsaken sons, husbands, brothers.

"Miss Butler is a committed pacifist," Mrs. Cobb said.

Miss Randolph gave a solemn nod. "As are many within the movement. Miss Butler, you might do well at the commune in Seneca Falls. Should you ever choose to return north."

"I have no interest in communal living," said Miss Butler. Her tone suggested that neither had she any interest in New York.

"We do well enough," Mrs. Cobb said, with a small smile. "Our newspaper's reach is limited, but there are a number of adherents in the area. We have an interest in publishing a book, perhaps. We found Mr. Davis's new gospels most interesting. The movement grows as God wills."

"We have strayed from the point," Miss Randolph said. Though she bore an academic interest in how the Spiritualists of St. Augustine conducted their affairs, a haunting required immediate attention. There would be time later, perhaps, for the sharing of mundanities. "As I understand it, many men and boys must have made Palm Brides on this November waning. What proof have you that any of them called down this spirit? That it is certainly due to Mr. Bradley's efforts?"

"We knew he was constructing one." Mrs. Cobb sipped her tea, her eyes slipping from Miss Randolph's face to a plate of shortbread. "He took our mare Stella to the pines a week past. Men often bring animals with them to the making of a Palm Bride—a horse, oxen, a dog. Their presence acts as a barrier between the man and any rousing power."

"Better to put down a possessed dog," Miss Butler said.

"Stella is quite well, God be praised," Mrs. Cobb concluded. "As interested in her feed bucket as ever. I once saw an ox driven by spirits. It's unsightly. A bloody affair."

Miss Randolph noted the mare's condition in her book. What a time the Seneca Falls group would have with this, this—*glut* of information, and little of it textbook or seemingly useful. She had never heard of animals used in such a fashion, only human mediums who performed what was required to communicate with the spirit.

"You have spoken to this Mr. Bradley, then?"

The two women's eyes met. They had a way about them, Miss Randolph observed, were quite communicative in their silences. She supposed two such must be.

"We don't want to spook him," Miss Butler said. "He's done nothing wrong, exactly. Certainly nothing the sheriff needs to know about."

"There's time yet," Mrs. Cobb said. "Tradition has it that should a Bride be constructed successfully, she comes to life on the Christmas full moon."

"There's no time," Miss Butler said. The corners of her firm mouth twitched, as though it pained her to disagree but would not keep her from soldiering on. "Jessamine, surely you see that it's already quick, this spirit. We can't wait until—"

Miss Randolph made a noise of disapproval. "Forgive my

bluntness, but this is why spirits must be dealt with in proper conditions. Séances conducted by experienced practitioners stand much less of a chance of—"

"Proper conditions?" Mrs. Cobb said. Her hands remained loosely wrapped around her teacup, her mouth smiling. A brow lifted, inquisitive. "If you've heard of us, Miss Randolph, we have also heard of you. We're aware of how some in New York conduct their spirits."

"Jessamine—"

But there was little use in Miss Butler's attempt. "Word came to us in the early days," Mrs. Cobb went on, "of a séance held outside Seneca Falls. Such a loosing of boundaries. Such carefree mediums and their lightly-held belief! Fourteen dead, was it? Ruled a mass suicide?" A sip of her tea, ruddy lips pursed on the cup's white rim. "Your districts brim with mischief, Miss Randolph. Yet here you are, as though your own house is in order."

Miss Randolph found herself without rebuttal.

"The voice you heard some nights past was not mine," Mrs. Cobb said, "nor Miss Butler's. That was hers."

On her word—perhaps, Miss Randolph marveled, at her command—the dining room's windows snapped open. Night air whirled in, rustling heavy brocade curtains, and brought it with an icy scent, colder than the balmy Florida autumn. *Clamminess & chill assoc. with the presence of spirits,* she jotted hastily, and then looked at the largest window. They all stared, the three women, and saw the Villa's courtyard: the half-broken Toledo tiles and the kitchen garden, the bench beneath a sheltering bay tree, the coquina walls overtaken by vines, and a figure moving among the Spanish bayonets.

***

Villa Reina was among the most haunted places Miss Randolph had experienced. She hadn't quite grasped it, in her first assessment; she'd been distracted by the exotic Spanish-style glamor, the unusual plant life, the self-possessed women within. She'd attributed the courtyard's quiet and the Villa's watchful air to its history, rather than its present.

There had been more violent manifestations, she allowed; there had been the Jacobs house in Poughquag, and one of the Cortland sessions in which a medium drew down, quite on accident, the spirit of an early settler, bloodthirsty and raving. There had been the meeting at her grandfather's home outside Seneca Falls, of which she occasionally still dreamt. But the house in St. Augustine was soaked in spirit—no doubt its property was too, if she ventured outside to make a full circuit around the grounds and groves—and quivering, nearly, poised on some precipice. Its faded grandeur carried ghosts in its bones. It inhabited the liminal slip between colonial past and shattered, war-bitten present. The locomotive winding through a thoroughly beaten South had given Miss Randolph more to chew on than she cared to swallow. At one point during the trip, she had drifted to sleep and woken abruptly, staring out the window, certain for the briefest of moments that she, too, had passed beyond... had been collecting departed spirits all along the way like pearls sewn into the train of a wedding gown... would arrive at the depot in Georgia to find herself at the world's edge, nothing more awaiting.

A lamp toppled from the mantel and, after just missing Miss Randolph's shoulder, shattered on the brick fronting the fireplace.

"Well!" she said. "A boisterous one."

"She was known in her time for a trickster," Mrs. Cobb said. "I'd thought to offer you a bed for the night—I'm sure you must be wearied—but... Mae, what do you think?"

Miss Butler did not turn from where she stood at the window. "The mare's gotten loose."

"What?"

"There's a light in the barn," Miss Butler continued. "But she's loose. Rampaging a bit." Now she did turn, just enough to cast pale eyes at Miss Randolph. "A funny thing, that. Your arrival seems to have precipitated some increase in spiritual activity."

"Mae," Mrs. Cobb said, with a note of reproach. She rose from her preparations at the table, her array of herb bundles and Bible and chalk, and went to the window. Miss Randolph saw no reason to note how Mrs. Cobb's hand slipped into Miss Butler's, their fingers twining and then hidden between voluminous folds of skirt. "Heaven's mercy! Has she a rider?"

"Not Wyn," Miss Butler said. Her voice seemed to be dwindling with each utterance in a slight but unmistakable concession to fear. "Is that a woman?"

It was no woman, Miss Randolph saw when she reached the large northern window, nor even a feminine shape aboard the mare's twisted back. She could not fault Miss Butler for inaccuracy: only rarely did two people perceive a spirit in the same manner. Even during the most standard of séances, when the dead person's identity was known, its spirit appeared different to each set of eyes.

The spirit at Villa Reina struck Miss Randolph as ageless, sexless. She did not understand how Mrs. Cobb could see it as specifically female, even given the Palm Bride's purpose and attributes. She saw nothing of a human form in the courtyard as the mare pranced and bucked, only a gathering darkness within the night, luminous and gravid in the same moment. It lay over the horse like a veil. It seemed to twine among her mane and tail, their blackness deepening and their hairs lifting, floating on the air. Her movements were stilted, precise and dainty, nothing Miss Randolph would have expected from a workhorse. Stiffness contorted her body, neck arched and hocks lifted high from the stones, in the manner of a horse drawn up tight under rein.

Miss Butler repeated the rosary under her breath and Miss Randolph thought, *Boston Irish*. Shame at her brief sally into judgment collapsed into fear as the mare outside the window danced near.

"You said," Miss Randolph murmured, "that animals are brought to the Palm Bride ritual, to act as a barrier between loose spirits and men."

"They are," Mrs. Cobb said. Her voice did not waver, which Miss Randolph admired. "If it works, the animal is frenzied and violent. This... I don't recognize it."

The mare stepped close and reared, and Miss Randolph found her hand on the window, clutching the sill for support. She almost envied Mrs. Cobb and Miss Butler—that they could cling to one another—that, after this conspicuous mess was resolved, they would have one another to comfort and be comforted. She forced her mind to details, for the night would be need to be transcribed as exactly as possible: the horse's alien movements, her eyes rolled white, her mane tangled and over-long, and blood trickling beneath the hair, streaked down her flanks like a Plains mount painted for war.

Yellow teeth gnashed when the mare's mouth opened, and

neither whicker nor neigh emerged, but only a faint echo of human laughter.

"This must be dealt with," Miss Randolph said. "We waste time. Come."

Turning from the window and its ghastly view, she made for her satchel, abandoned near her vacant chair. She longed to flee upstairs to some musty guest room, or perhaps retreat to the Villa's kitchen, tuck small potatoes into the fire until they whistled inside their jackets and slice bread with extravagant butter. Instead she rebuked herself for weakness, for capitulating to distress and allowing the soft air in St. Augustine to go to work on her, slowing her blood and whispering of ease. She took up the chalk Mrs. Cobb had left and began marking the table's burnished surface. The rote motions gave her peace, or at least stilled the tremor in her hands, built bulwarks against the sense of creeping wrong permeating the night. It was not just the sight of the mare that troubled her; it was the voice that had shattered her sleeping mind not five days past, and it was the landscape that slid from destruction into utter wreck and decay the further away from New York she went, and it was the scent on the coast road, blood ground into the very earth, yielding God knew what fruits, and it was the presence that had overtaken the horse, that wisp blacker than the surrounding night, that invisible hand on reins that did not exist.

The women settled themselves in their chairs once more. Miss Butler was quite gray. Miss Randolph took it upon herself to pour the last of the cold tea into her cup. Eyes downcast, Mrs. Cobb said, "Perhaps we've indeed left it too late. Perhaps we were too—"

"It is never too late until you're dead," Miss Randolph said briskly, and chuckled. "Even then, I'm sure the present company know such matters to be up for debate."

The two women looked at her in one startled movement, and then at one another. Some color came back into Miss Butler's cheeks. Miss Randolph held out her hands. "Shall we begin?

***

The dining room was suffused with a quality Miss Randolph knew well: a certain tightness to the air, a pressure within the sockets of her eyes and the joints of her limbs, as though hands gripped her throat. Nails dug into her palm, and she could not discern whether they belonged to her or to Miss Butler on her left.

"Wyndham Ezekiel Bradley," Mrs. Cobb said. Her voice was quiet and measured, but Miss Randolph felt it to the nerves of her teeth. She knew that members of the movement in New York, perhaps as far away as Chicago or New Orleans, would feel it—would awake in the night and wonder. "Relinquish your hold on matter not of this world."

A banishing, in its usual state, was nothing more than a reversal of the séance ceremony. But that was suitable only for dealing with the spirits of the dead. This spirit, so far as Mrs. Cobb indicated, had never been alive in the mortal sense. *She commands the dead,* Mrs. Cobb had said, *she is not one of them.*

Beyond the northern window, light moved in the courtyard. It was neither lamp nor torch but a ghost light, pale and preternaturally steady, a glimmering seed growing in the pines.

"Ada Nuit—" Mrs. Cobb continued, and Miss Butler gasped.

"Jessamine, no! To name her—you'd give her too much power."

Miss Randolph would have voiced her agreement, had a voracious presence not invaded her mind and body. She had been prepared for such an occurrence, as mediums must be, but it was never pleasant. Power was many things, but never pleasant. Her own spirit soared up, and she watched her body go rigid in its seat. Her head tipped to one side and then the other, eyes rolling as though seeking their usual pilot, and her mouth gaped wide.

"I am not yours to command, but I come when called."

A clatter sounded, the dining room's door flung open. The man stood there: Wyn Bradley, flushed and fever-eyed, large hands knotted around a bundle of palm fronds and bark which Miss Randolph recognized as the remnants of his ritual. He looked from Miss Butler to Mrs. Cobb, and finally at Miss Randolph, with no hint of recognition.

"Wyn," Mrs. Cobb said, gently. "This error must be undone." She did not loose Miss Randolph's hand but lifted it, with seeming difficulty. "You in your ignorance have—"

"Ignorance?" Wyn barked, and advanced toward the table. Miss Randolph observed Miss Butler shrinking, her hand quivering and bloodless. Mrs. Cobb's deep brown skin had lost a touch of its luster. She wondered at the fear of the two women, and at own her puzzlement; naturally an unexpected and powerful spirit was to be feared, but this man? He was tall, but bore the marks of privation on his body. He was angry, but the wisdom and spiritual strength of the movement's adherents prevailed beyond that. His face twisted, gleaming-red, as he bent down to Mrs. Cobb. "It's you who are ignorant. You witches, holed up here like queens—you play at power and you have none of it. You believe you can take her away?"

"I come when called," the voice that was not Miss Randolph's repeated. "I am not yours to command."

A light broke over Wyn's face, white and will-o-the-wisp, a flicker of the presence outside the window now bursting through the courtyard. The mare paced in its midst, pawing at the stones. "My bride," he said reverently, his eyes moving to Miss Randolph's frozen face. "You've come."

"Ada Nuit," Mrs. Cobb said, and stood from her chair. She did not release Miss Randolph's or Miss Butler's hands, though the latter looked near to fainting. "Chaperone of souls, you will depart this body and this house."

"I am not yours to command."

"She belongs to me!" Wyn cried. "Don't think to—"

"Ada Nuit," Mrs. Cobb continued, inexorable. "Mistress of deception, you bear your name well. You will depart this body and this house."

She lifted her arms and Miss Butler stood too, the pair of them dragging at Miss Randolph's hands as her body began to thrash. Wyn crouched beside her, openly weeping. He lifted the Palm Bride toward her like an offering. "You won't leave me! I prayed, I called, oh how I prayed and you—"

"I come when called."

"Ada Nuit," Mrs. Cobb said, and Miss Randolph's floating spirit marveled that her voice rang against the bookshelves and sideboard, without the slightest alteration in pitch. "Night queen, wanderer, light of hand. You will depart this body and this house, and go away on your corpse roads. You will flee this body and this house, never again to set foot inside Villa Reina."

"I am not yours to command," the spirit within Miss Randolph roared, and her body burst up from the chair.

Miss Butler was flung backward and Mrs. Cobb staggered on her feet, and Wyn—Wyn, Miss Randolph observed with distant disgust, threw his arms around her shoulders. That such a presence could have been roused at his behest—that a spirit so powerful would respond, even sidelong, to weakness and greedy spite—

The palm dolly dropped from his grasp, bark fibers scattering across the table.

"She belongs to me," he said again, peering into Miss Randolph's face with large, wet eyes. "She must stay with me. I called and here she is, and none of you have a damn thing to do with it."

Laughter echoed in the dining room, shades of the same light, mocking voice that had emanated from the mare's mouth. Miss Randolph watched her body push Wyn aside as though he weighed no more than an infant. He dropped to one knee, palms upturned and imploring. "I come when called," the spirit told him, loving and final. "I am not yours to command."

"You are mine!" He clutched at her skirt, and Miss Randolph noted how creased it was, travel-worn and dusty. "Don't leave me again, leave me to the mercy of these witches, this Yankee bitch—"

"Ada Nuit." Mrs. Cobb's voice returned with its full force and deepened to a thrum, a pulse that traveled on the air like lightning into a metal rod. She raised a hand to the rim of her turban, which had begun to unravel, and it came loose, revealing black braids woven crown-like around her skull. "Lonesome walker, you will depart this body and this house. You will carry your retinue elsewhere, for your souls are not welcome here."

"My souls have always been here," Miss Randolph's guest

replied, and the woman herself felt her spirit reel in response. If she lingered too long outside her body, it became possible—even likely—that she would join that retinue, go traipsing through the godforsaken marshes and lych ways of Florida, ever bound to this spirit's will. *Ada Nuit,* she thought, and allowed herself a shiver at the name. "My souls were among the first people of this shore, and among the conquering hordes, and among those who called themselves holy. You cannot set your foot down, Jessamine Parvenu, but that you tread upon the shadow you would banish."

The ghost light in the dining room wavered as another glow bloomed. Mrs. Cobb's face shone, sweat beading on her forehead. She brought the ends of the strip of blue fabric together, knotting them swiftly into a complicated knot. Miss Randolph watched her head jerk, eyes bulging, and wished herself safely cocooned within her own skeleton, in control of its faculties. Why, after all, had the spirit chosen her to inhabit? Why not Mrs. Cobb, surely more familiar and more suited to a presence of this land, or Miss Butler, more pliant? She struggled for a grip on the material world, an anchor to keep her in the earthly sphere, and found only shifting sand beneath her spirit's feet.

"Hence," Mrs. Cobb commanded. Her hands on the turban throbbed in Miss Randolph's faint vision, gnarl-knuckled and straining. "Back, Ada Nuit, out and away. There is no place for you here."

Miss Randolph would not have credited it to Miss Butler—but the pale woman moved to where Wyn's manikin lay on the table. She snatched it and dashed with it toward the fireplace. It was the work of a moment before Wyn caught her up, his arms enclosing her shoulders and waist, for naught. The Palm Bride landed in the midst of burning logs and caught, for what was it after all,

Miss Randolph reflected, but a bundle of kindling? What was any woman but coarse matter fit only for fueling another's flame?

A shriek rose, and Miss Randolph expected to see it issuing from her own mouth, for surely Ada Nuit felt the destruction of her idol. Instead she sank back into her body as the invading spirit diminished, blood throbbing in her limbs when sensation returned. Miss Butler thrashed free, crashing onto hands and knees before the fireplace. It was Wyn screaming, she noted only when Mrs. Cobb caught her arm: Wyn, howling fit for a demon's choir as flame engulfed him.

Gobbets of fire dripped from the ends of his fair hair, caught at his shirtsleeves and ate their way through his trousers, and he screamed. His voice remained in the dining room long after Miss Randolph believed it should have fled, a shade of its strength and pain, like a fingerprint on clean glass.

"I didn't..." Miss Butler said, her voice hoarse with smoke. "I didn't know what would—I didn't think that—"

Lines carved down from Mrs. Cobb's nose, her mouth tired and sad. "What more was there to be done, beloved?"

"What did she call you?" Miss Randolph said. If they were not going to be courteous and ask after her condition—well. It was an occupational hazard. She had not arrived to St. Augustine believing this would be a pleasure trip, though the vaunted hospitality of Southerners left something to be desired. "Par—what was it?"

"An insult," Mrs. Cobb said, "and a weak one." She surveyed the corpse on her dining room floor. "I can't recall a time when women were not left to clean up a mess."

***

When Annabel Randolph departed Villa Reina it was full sun, the air a parting kiss on her cheek. Despite the pleasant temperature she thought she would not miss the flowering coast— its solitary wise women, its gray shades, its offensive amount of winter flora—and greeted the thought of several days' train trip with pleasure. There was a proper way to do things; there was a proper round of seasons, evidenced by her own New York, currently in the grip of ice and snow; there was a set of principles to be applied to the work of spirits, and look what happened when those were ignored. She patted her notebook where its thick cover bulged the satchel's pocket, reassuring herself of the facts.

Ada Nuit, if the spirit truly deserved a name of such grandeur, was banished. Whatever unwelcome grip she'd had, briefly, upon Miss Randolph's self left naught but a faint headache, chased away by bed and strong coffee. She was herself once more, back straight and skirt brushed clean, correct in manner and thought, firm against Florida's vagaries of sunshine and long-ranging spirits. By the time she reached Seneca Falls, Ada Nuit's presence would diminish entirely, into the realms of academia and theory, to be discussed in measured tones. She carried back knowledge, the fruits of effort and the growth of wisdom, and Villa Reina—

Villa Reina retained only the ghosts of its own past.

She paused outside the gates, recalling her first glimpse of the manor through iron and vine. There had been a man allowing her entrance, and now his remains lay in the Huguenot cemetery. Now the courtyard was calm and leaf-swept, sun glinting on glass panes in the distance, behind which, she thought, Mrs. Cobb and Miss Butler were going about the business of the movement in their own ways. Now nothing moved within the gates but a faint whisper of shadow sliding dark through the Spanish bayonets.

There's No Need to Fear the Darkness

Heather Morris

Heather Morris is a cyborg librarian living in North Carolina. Her work has appeared in Apex Magazine, Strange Horizons, and Daily Science Fiction, among other places. You can find her on Twitter @NotThatHeatherM

"So, do you have kids?" the detective asked, interrupting Brenda's reading to slide a cup of coffee across the table to her. While the coffee was welcome, she wasn't sure yet it was worth the interruption. She put her index finger flat against the last word she'd processed and looked up, blinking against the antiseptic light.

"What was that?"

She honestly hadn't even noticed that he'd left the room on his coffee run, or when exactly he'd returned. He stood with his back to the light to seem mysterious, he kept his feet instead of sitting because he wanted to appear tall and powerful as opposed to ingratiating or friendly. Yet the questions were friendly, or designed to seem so. As if he couldn't decide whether he should play good cop or bad cop, when in reality he didn't need to do either.

He was very, very new at this job.

"Do you have kids?" He fiddled with the lid of his own paper coffee cup.

"I'm not sure how that's relevant, Detective—?" she took a sip of the coffee; it definitely wasn't worth the interruption.

"Hernandez." Even if she couldn't read the emotion all over his face, his voice was saturated with it. Pure annoyance; he had probably told her his name five times at least in the midst of all his incessant small talk, and he was also still sulking because she wasn't the great Cade Novak. As if Cade would have ever dragged his camera crew out here to the ass-end of nowhere for some little case that couldn't even drum up much local media enthusiasm.

Yes, he was very new at this.

"I'm just trying to make conversation," the detective sulked, when she failed to respond with the pleasantries he thought he deserved.

Brenda flipped the file closed; it was clear she wasn't getting back to it any time soon. Anyway, she had most of what she needed, and with luck the Blank would fill in the rest.

"No, I do not have any children." The socially expected response, the *do you?*, danced just out of reach. No need to ask. He was the kind of man who needed constant validation, and she wasn't going to reward that with social niceties.

"It's a kid, you know. The—the, uh, Blank."

"I'm aware of that, yes."

"Well, that's why I brought it up." He prickled with defensiveness. "It bothers some people. Kids can be rough."

"I've worked with juvenile Blanks before. Is the coroner is ready for us? By all means, let's be on our way."

"But you haven't finished the file."

That was his own fault, of course, but Brenda simply shrugged.

"I'd rather not drag this out further than necessary. There are a lot of cases on my list to get through."

Actually, there weren't. For the first time in weeks, she didn't have another job on the line. But people were always dying, and for all she knew there would be something waiting for her before this one was done.

The detective scowled, not quite buying her little lie. "Are all Lazes so..." he didn't fill in the blank, allowing her to supplement with all sorts of interesting adjectives.

"Difficult?"

"Sure. *Difficult.*"

Brenda scooped up the beige file folder and tossed the remains of the mediocre coffee into a nearby trash can.

"There're only the three of us, so the sample size is rather limited, I'm afraid. Also, please don't call me a Laz. I've never understood that term, and I don't like it."

"Laz? It's short for Lazarus, the—"

Generally Brenda slouched through life, but the detective was too short for this effort to make much difference, so she stretched to her full height and pushed past him into the hallway.

"I know who Lazarus was, Detective. But, in case it has escaped you thus far, Lazarus was the dead man. The one who brought him back to life was God."

There. Cade and Aage were always saying that if she didn't want to be dismissed so easily, she had to be a little shocking. Well, that was shocking.

It was also petty, and rather mean-spirited. But she'd had a long, lonely month, and there was a dead kid waiting on a table to meet her, and the detective was right about one thing. Kids were rough. She couldn't dredge up fake smiles or false enthusiasm, so petty and mean-spirited would have to do.

***

Cade was the one who came up with the term Laz, of course, in those first heady days after they all came crashing together with such unanticipated force. Brenda and Aage would have been content to coast under the radar forever, ignoring their strange new abilities, but Cade wanted more out of life. Even after less than seventy two hours, they all knew these things about each other with an instinct that terrified and exhilarated in equal measure.

"What we need is a superhero team name," Cade had said, dreamily, staring up at Aage's watermarked motel-room ceiling as if *The Creation of Adam* was painted there.

Aage clambered over him, searching for his Winstons with one hand and his lighter with the other. "Christ's sake, we're not *superheroes.*"

"No? Got another word for it? Those things will kill you, you know."

A shrug. "Die young, stay pretty."

He, of course, was their elder, already graying at the temples, and the smoking did no favors for his skin. Still, already he had hooked his claws into Brenda's heart. Love. *Love.* What kind of insanity was that?

"Brenda, darling, please help me convince Mr. Lund that we'd rather have him old and ugly than gorgeous in the grave, and that those cigarettes make him stink abominably, and that we should have a superhero name. Oh, and stretchy outfits."

Brenda plucked the cigarette from between Aage's slim fingers for an illicit drag before smashing it beyond redemption in the bedside ashtray.

"I draw the line at stretchy outfits. He's right. We're not superheroes."

"We can bring people *back to life*. That sounds like a genuine superpower to me."

"For about thirty five seconds," Aage argued. "Gibbering and disoriented."

"So we'll get better at it. We'll practice."

"On who, exactly?"

"Everyone dies, Aage. *Until now*." Cade's eyes sparkled. "When people find out about us, they'll be lined up for miles to get our help."

"When people find out about us they'll say we're possessed by demons, or try to vivisect us for the sake of science. It's not a useful service. It's a party trick. A *frightening* party trick."

"So we get out ahead of it, spin it. Name ourselves, brand ourselves. How about the Reanimators?"

"That," Aage flopped back to the mattress with a dramatic thud, "is terrible."

Cade scrunched up his nose, which made Brenda laugh and want to kiss him. So she did.

Cade hardly noticed. "Maybe there's a term about zombies we can use. You know, voodoo."

Aage didn't like that idea, either. "Problematic. Cultural appropriation. Also, zombies frighten people. They're already going to be terrified of us."

"Will not."

"Will so."

"You are so contrarian. Oh, I've got it. Aage, Brenda, Cade...we can be the ABCs!"

"What are we, a kid's variety cartoon? Also, darling, that would put you last in line, and we all know that's unsustainable in the long term."

Aage was right about that, too.

But Cade was on a roll now, and he just barreled right through the criticism. "Something about the underworld. Death. Hades. Persephone? Oh, I know. Lazarus!"

"Lazarus was brought back, he wasn't the bringer."

"I know, I know. Look, the two of you can lecture me on the semantic difference between Frankenstein and Frankenstein's monster—"

"Creature!" Brenda and Aage's protest was immediate, and in unison.

"Fine, *creature*, later. It's catchy. We make up a hashtag, do some visible miracle working, crash boom bang: superheroes."

"I don't understand you," Aage groused. "Isn't this miracle enough?"

By *this* he meant *them*, the improbability and the exhilaration of all that they had been in only three days, how much more they could be.

But nothing was ever enough for Cade. That was how he'd set off such sparks in Brenda and Aage in the first place.

Within twenty minutes he had a clunky hashtag that he was trying his damndest to get trending. He started circulating rumors, some spotted with truth, others outright fantasy, about people who'd died sudden deaths leaving messages beyond the grave. Within two days, a prominent content aggregator was posting listicles like "Ten Famous Corpses Who MUST Be Reanimated by the Lazarus." A few days after that, suicidal teens on a message board started trading tips on how to make sure that the Laz—even at this point, everyone still thought the three of them were one figure—chose them for reanimation, or didn't. That's when Brenda really started to worry. She remembered being a suicidal teen on message boards, couldn't stomach having any part in inspiring such behavior. But spin it, Cade said, and if it didn't bother him then she felt like wasn't allowed to let it bother her. So they spun and they spun and they spun, trying to work out a course while the race was already in progress.

A month later, Cade Novak brought the President of the United States back to life for three minutes and fourteen seconds after an undetected brain aneurysm felled her during an economy speech in Quincy. The incident was caught from a dozen angles, streamed live across the world. She stumbled through the next few lines of her speech, and then she said "Why is everyone so quiet?," and then she started to sing a gospel hymn, halting but clear. Then she whispered something to Cade, and then she died for the second time.

And nothing was ever the same.

***

The coroner of this county was a soft-chinned Black woman who introduced herself as Kate Allen. Her space was cramped and cluttered; shoved out of sight so that the living didn't have to think about the dead more than was strictly necessary. Brenda appreciated her brisk efficiency, her lack of small talk. The Blank's small body was already laid out beneath a sheet on the examination table. "Shall we?" Allen said after the introductions were past, gesturing to the body. Hernandez nodded affirmation.

"Wait," Brenda said, holding up a hand to stay them. "First, I need to be clear that you both understand what is going to happen here."

"I sat in on a lecture by Mr. Lund in Portland last spring," Allen said.

There would have been a couple hundred people in that lecture hall, but at least she had seen it in real time. Brenda gave a slight nod, and turned.

"Detective Hernandez?"

"I've read the book. And of course I watched all the training tapes when you were raised as a possible assistant for this case."

The tapes. Hah. Like the training tapes looked any different to him than the latest summer superhero movie. Cheaper, if anything.

Brenda straightened her spine, folding her hands behind her back.

"Alright, here's how it goes. I will resuscitate the Blank. I will ask the questions that I've deemed appropriate from the list provided by you, Detective. But I will not lead the subject in any way. I will not coach them into an answer you want or are expecting to hear. Sometimes they are coherent. Sometimes they are not. I will do the best I can to inspire coherence. You will not speak."

Detective Hernandez was not at all pleased with that. "I—"

"Will not speak."

Allen flashed Hernandez a look, and his aggression subsided into a nod. Brenda affected not to notice either, the aggression or the submission.

"Given the Blank's age at time of death, and the trauma involved, I anticipate about forty five seconds. I will try to push that based on the Blank's level of coherence and cooperation, but when it's done, it's done. I won't drag the poor thing back twice." She couldn't, actually, but no one needed to know that part. "Whether it solves your case or not, what they give is what you get. Clear?"

"As crystal," Hernandez said between his teeth. Then, belatedly, "Ma'am." As if that pause would bother her, somehow.

"Good. Now, you've taken all the trace you need from the body?"

"We have your fingerprints and DNA on file," Allen said, her turn to be less-than-pleased. No one liked that Lazes refused to wear gloves.

"There's no telling what my touch could disturb or destroy. Are you done with trace on this body, or do I need to come back tomorrow?"

"We're done."

"Fine. You may proceed."

Allen folded down the sheet, and Brenda took in her first glimpse of Milo Hunter Simonson, seven and a half, deceased for sixty seven hours, the best candidate for resuscitation from a multiple homicide with sparse physical evidence and few solid leads.

Best candidate because he was the only victim who's skull was still intact.

His skin would once have been called caramel or some similarly ridiculously insensitive food term, but now it resembled nothing more than wet, dense sand. Corkscrew curls, longer than Brenda was used to seeing on little boys, crowned his tiny head. His thin, naked clavicle was studded with bruises like dull blue jewels and she could see the ghost of fingers encircling his throat.

For just one second, Brenda closed her eyes.

After she opened them again, she slid her right hand beneath the Blank's fragile neck and touched the bare skin at the base of his hairline.

He took a deep, gasping breath.

"Mommy? Mommy!"

Aage had been the one to note that pre-adolescent kids tended to regress when they were dead. This Blank sounded like he was about four.

Brenda softened her voice for the lie. "Your mommy's in the next room, getting you some apple juice."

A wheezing, nasal whine. "I want lemonade."

"She's getting you lemonade."

"She is?"

"She is. Honey, can you tell me your name, please?"

His little face screwed up tight. His dull irises had once been brown.

"Milo Hunter."

"What's your favorite toy, Milo?"

In the corner of Brenda's eye, Hernandez looked aghast at the seemingly pointless question. He even tapped his watch in a comic pantomime. But at least he was keeping quiet.

The boy laughed, suddenly delighted by some flash of memory or outside stimulus. "Ginny Bear!"

"Yeah? I'll have your mommy get you Ginny Bear."

His lip contorted in a pout. "Ginny Bear has a hole in her eye."

Someone had come into his house, and they had done unspeakable things to this child and his family, and they had even shot his fucking teddy bear.

Brenda hated her job.

She kept her voice soft, lightly curious. "Who put the hole there, Milo?"

"Uncle. The dark tastes like pennies."

Milo did not have any biological uncles. His father had a list of known associates, many of them petty criminals, who might have fit the bill, though. If that was how the child was able to express the last person he saw, Brenda would have to run with it.

"What did Uncle say when he put the hole in Ginny Bear's eye?"

"Bad words. And nothing. I'm thirsty."

"I know, honey, I know." With her free hand, Brenda stroked those soft curls, using a hopefully familiar touch sensation to keep him anchored and calm.

"Are you a daddy or are you a mommy?" he asked. Oh yeah, he had definitely regressed. His world was a small binary, and he had to fit Brenda into it.

"I'm a girl, like your mommy."

"Mommy has a hole in her hand. It's red and she yelled."

"Do you know how she got the hole in her hand?"

"A bang bang gun. Luca likes playing spaceman but Mommy won't let him pretend guns cause they are bad."

Luca was his nine-year-old brother, in one of the cold storage freezers stacked on the far wall. The Blank's eyes rolled back and forth in his head. Brenda tried to stabilize her grip on him, her palm itching with sweat.

"Did you see Mommy get the hole or just hear her yell?"

"I'm thirsty. Bug told me to shut up, little bitch. The dark smells thick."

"Did you see anyone before you closed your eyes?"

"Bug, and Teo close up. I want *lemonade*. My throat hurts. Luca's hiding under the bed but I didn't tell so you have to promise not to."

"Did you hear Bug or Teo say anything to your daddy or your mommy?"

"Bang bang. Daddy said a big bad word with a f. Can you hear the dark inside your ears?"

Brenda's fingers had begun to go numb. She twitched them against the Blank's neck and he giggled. "Spiders tickle."

Not much time left.

"Milo, what did you see before you closed your eyes?"

"Red holes. Daddy was sleeping on his stomach. Bug looked mean. He—pulled..."

The connection sizzled and snapped. Brenda lowered the Blank's head back to the table, flexing her fingers to get the feeling back. Kate Allen had tears in the corners of her eyes, and Detective Hernandez looked ashen. Allen resettled the sheet over the body.

"I would assume that Bug and Teo are Miguel and Mateo Ortega," Brenda said, to get them back on track. "I can't say with one hundred percent certainty that they were the last people he saw, but I would certainly recommend you start there."

Hernandez swallowed hard. "What...what was all that about the dark?"

"Irrelevant. I thought you watched the tapes, Detective. They always talk about the dark, and those are statements we can categorically set aside."

"He was thirsty," Allen said, soft as a sigh.

"Damage to the throat. I couldn't say why he was strangled while the others were shot. You'd have to consult a behavioral analyst about that, or ask one of the offenders themselves. I sincerely hope this gives you what you need, Detective."

"I...yes...that is...I think we can work with it. Thank you."

"I'm glad to be of assistance. Remember, the Blank's testimony cannot be used in any legal action, but if you do get to that stage I will be able to testify to what I heard today." Criminal lawyers universally hated the Lazes, of course, because the precedents were still being argued, but as long as they allowed her to take the stand she would do it. *That*, she constantly argued with Cade, was the real superpower. Not the resuscitative spark, but what they did with it once the restless dead were lost again to the dark.

Hernandez looked at her, and then his eyes slid away. He was afraid of her. They always were, afterwards.

Brenda's stomach felt like curdled milk. She asked for the washroom, and went to scrub all trace of the child from her skin.

***

As soon as she was back in her hotel room Brenda kicked off her shoes and curled like a pill bug in the center of the absurdly plush mattress and wept.

Give him credit, it was Cade who called her first. Well, Aage had more trouble figuring out time zones, and he might not even know where she was. Come to think of it, even *she* wasn't sure where she was. Alabama? Georgia?

Somewhere in the South, anyway.

"I never, never, *never* want a kid," Brenda wailed at Cade, instead of saying hello.

Aage was the one who had been bringing up the idea of surrogacy or adoption lately; casually and cautiously, as if it didn't really concern him, though they all knew that for a lie. Cade was indifferent, Brenda was opposed. But Cade knew they weren't really talking about their own potential kids right now, they were really talking about the Blank, about Milo Hunter Simonson, seven and half and dead. He talked her down, half-heard platitudes and soothing sounds filtered through the phone speaker, though what she really needed was someone to touch her.

She could go out and find someone. Neither Cade nor Aage would much mind. But it didn't seem like a good idea. Not in the damn South.

"He said the dark tasted like pennies. *Blood*, Cade. You know that's what it means. His darkness tastes like blood."

"Shh. Shh. Look, take a few days, come out to California. I'll get Lund down here somehow."

"I don't want California. I want home."

"This is home."

"*Your* home."

"Damn it, Brenda, you want to have this fight again *now*?"

"I want people to stop murdering children. I want to live in a place without cameras following me around every corner. That's what I want."

He was doing his stupid docudrama, or whatever he was calling it these days because *reality TV* sounded too tawdry. This was probably going to end up the plotline of one of the episodes. She didn't want to fight, didn't want to give him the ammunition, so she just hung up, and he let her and didn't try back.

When Aage finally called, a long time later, she just let the phone buzz against her heart, didn't even make an attempt to answer. He had to know how tired she was. She could feel his worry, but she couldn't rise to meet it.

Fortunately, there was an overabundance of light in the hotel room. Two bedside lamps, two standing lamps in the opposite corners, the buzzing florescence of the bathroom light, track lighting above the bed. With all of them on, eventually she managed to fall asleep.

***

The recently dead are preoccupied with many different things. The last song they heard on the radio. Complaints about the weather. Odd aches and pains that they can't seem to pin down. The names of their loved ones. The names of their enemies.

But all of them, *all of them*, in their brief second chance at life, speak of the dark.

That was almost the first thing Cade, Aage, and Brenda figured out, when they finally had a chance to compare notes.

The very first thing they'd figured out was the improbable timeline. How at almost the same exact moment in three different cities thousands of miles apart, they had all unexpectedly discovered that they could wake the dead.

Aage learned at the side of his grandmother's hospice bed. She'd been unresponsive for hours, it was only a matter of time, but when he held her hand he felt a tug, and then his grandmother sat up, shouting something about Uncle Jokum and spoons. Startled, he'd tried to let go, but she sunk her nails into his skin with a strength she hadn't possessed in years. When he finally broke the contact, she collapsed with a deflating sigh. Only later did he learn that she'd been dead for some minutes before he unthinkingly reached out for her hand.

Aage buried his grandmother, but something was still tugging, and so he travelled south and west.

Cade learned when he came home from a house-painting job itching for a shower and instead found his boyfriend twisted up beside an empty bottle of pills. No note, no explanation. Cade never talked about it in any depth, but Brenda and Aage know how it went all the same. Fumbling for the phone, a moan that can't quite yet figure out how to turn into a scream, cradling the boy's too-stiff body, and then the *spark*.

"Babe, the pancakes burned," the boy said, his eyelashes fluttering.

Cade gawped, incredulous. He'd been wrong; there was still time.

Then, "The dark tastes like smoke. Sing air mattress. Owls dance chilly shallot. Sorry sorry sorry sorry love love love."

And Cade buried his boy, but something was still tugging, and so he travelled east.

Brenda only lost her dog.

But, no. *Only* was not at all the right word, it was too diminishing, and she had to get better at accepting the validity of her emotions. Because Dandelion was more important to her at that point in her life than any human being had been for years. And when she saw him curled up at the end of her bed and known he wasn't breathing something had shattered.

Then she reached out to stroke his head one last time, and the *something* tugged, and her dead dog barked and shuddered.

Brenda buried Dandelion in her backyard even though it was against the city codes and then she rented out her house and then she travelled north.

A year and a day. That was what made it magic instead of

science, wasn't it? A year and a day alone in the wilderness, and then a brand new life.

For a year they each wandered, on trains and buses and airplanes. They ate in shitty chain restaurants and quiet backroad diners. They took pictures on their phones but did not share them with anyone. They drained their savings accounts and slept with strangers and got tattooed and snuck into movie theaters and got high with teenagers and stared at the threads coming from their fingertips which no one else seemed to see and they pretended that they were still young and they kept following the tug because there was nothing else worth doing anymore.

And then the day. In an art museum in a city none of them had ever seen before, they walked down three separate corridors, came together from three directions. And they weren't fixed, they weren't healed, but they knew each other, instinctively. Without a word, they *knew*. And it should have been enough.

***

The morning after Milo, Brenda got up early. She took her pills, spent extra time on her make-up and hair, pretended to read the free newspaper while she attempted to eat the hotel breakfast downstairs. The eggs tasted like old rubber.

There was a kid, maybe two or three years old, staring at her from a table across the room.

Little kids stared. They didn't have ulterior motives for doing so, they were just soaking up stimuli. And that was okay. Brenda flipped the page.

Milo's case wasn't mentioned in the paper. The initial details of the crime would have been reported on a few days before, and Detective Hernandez wouldn't release anything about the information Brenda had acquired unless they needed public assistance in finding the new suspects. She would have thought, with kids involved, the case would be a local sensation. But apparently Milo and Luca Simonson weren't the type of kids this town cared about.

Instead, Brenda read about a new dog park's grand opening, the local high school football team facing off against their archrivals, imminent rain.

She thought about California.

Whenever they were in California, Cade was the star and Brenda was the freak show. Somehow, Aage always managed to bypass the whole circus altogether. She kind of hated him for that, but she couldn't say she blamed him.

But it had been a long month. With Aage on his hospital tour and Cade filming the docudrama that kept their bills paid (they couldn't *charge* for resuscitation; that would be vile), Brenda had been the one crossing the continent to do the daily dirty work, visiting police department after police department, helping them to solve their never-ending lists of crime. There was little enough she could do. Bodies never sparked after four days—no cold cases would be getting solved by her touch. Often the dead were recalcitrant, reluctant to speak, or just downright unintelligible. No matter how many Blanks she woke, it would never be enough, she could never do enough, and after a month straight of hotel food and airport security lines, she was overwhelmed by the emptiness of it all.

Maybe even tired enough for California.

She'd collect Aage first, if he would cancel an appearance or two, and they could try to surprise Cade. As long as nothing came up before they got to him. No high profile, suspect-less murders or sudden deaths of wealthy celebrities without wills. A few quiet days, that was all she needed. Please, universe, a few quiet days.

She went back to her room to pack up and book the necessary tickets. But there was something else to do first, something she'd avoided the day before when the spark that woke Milo had left her too vulnerable and raw.

She kept a composition notebook in the inner pocket of her suitcase. She wouldn't keep this information digitally; it was too easy to be hacked, and everything they did was already scrutinized by the internet down to the smallest detail. This was a record just for the three of them, though Cade didn't often care to look and even Aage, despite his obsession with datasets and analyzing and improving their craft, thought Brenda's preoccupation was perverse.

Inside the notebook in her precise handwriting there were one thousand eight hundred and seventy four names.

Sofie Lund ; the dark sounds like clacking spoons.

Nathaniel Coleman ; the dark tastes like smoke.

And on and on and on and on.

Beside number one thousand eight hundred and seventy five, Brenda wrote *Milo Hunter Simonson ; the dark tastes like pennies, the dark smells thick, audial {?}*.

It was rare for a Blank to communicate the dark in two ways. The dark felt yellow, or it sounded like steam, or it tasted muddy, or it smelled hot. Only ten or a dozen Blanks had made multiple observations, all of those in the last three months. Brenda wondered if that meant that they were getting better at what they did—holding the connections longer, helping the Blanks communicate more clearly—or if it meant that the dark was getting stronger. If they'd inadvertently opened a door that could be accessed from both sides.

No one they'd awoken had yet spoken of anything resembling heaven or hell. No pearly gates or lakes of fire. Only the dark, unrelenting and infinitely variable.

Brenda put away the notebook, and rubbed at her tired eyes until afterimages bloomed against her eyelids.

There was so much to do. People died every minute of every day, a never-ending tide. But there had to be meaning behind what they had become. The dark had to be something classifiable, understandable. There had to be an answer that Brenda was capable of finding.

But in the meantime: packing, plane tickets. Aage, then California and Cade, some time to breathe freely with the people she loved. She did not need to think of the dark as an intelligent, hostile thing. She did not need to wonder what her own darkness would contain. She would find that out some other day.

On Your Honor

Kat Weaver

Kat Weaver is an artist who writes sometimes, or a writer who sometimes makes art. Her short stories in Lackington's (Issue 15, Summer 2017) and Apex Magazine. Her illustrations have accompanied stories in Lackington's, The Toast, Metaphorosis, the World Fantasy Award-winning She Walks in Shadows anthology, and Crossed Genres: Hidden Youth. She lives in Minneapolis with her girlfriend and two birds. Her portfolio website can be found at http://kathrynmweaver.com.

Paseia takes care to observe her supplicants before every consultation; a successful interpreter must read and accommodate any mood.

Fortunately, Lady Ouridia Diphan and Lady Biota Leanax descend from their shuttle in high spirits, which gain altitude as Paseia leads their ladyships to the appointed room. They are a pair in their early thirties, fiancées, both of them pretty as puddings straight from the mold. Though tall Lady Biota wears spectacles, and though Lady Ouridia has neglected to powder her freckles, their styles of dress and speech are otherwise nigh identical not only to each other, but to every other wealthy woman whom Paseia has served. Their gowns bell from this or that season's new waist-line; their hats perch upon the inevitable curls; their lips shape each syllable with gushing precision. The oracles, oh, just look at them!

Paseia, too, could rhapsodize about the parrots, but she will not subject their ladyships to the interpreters' orisons, most of which are fond insults and complaints.

Most oracles they pass are larger birds: their feet dry bracelets around their interpreters' forearms, their eyes big cabochons in leathery sockets, their crests raised with the eloquence of an actor's brow. Charmed-I'm-Sure, a scarlet beauty familiar to Paseia, thrusts her nubbin of a tongue into her interpreter's nostrils. On another woman's shoulder, a cockatoo intently cracks its beak into a block of wood; splinters trail the interpreter's skirts.

The Ladies Ouridia and Biota are enchanted, and Paseia cannot fault them. One does not see animal life except on planetside estates, or natural preserves, or on the zooships of Polukallista—not that Paseia has ever received an invitation to any of these extravagant locations—or on an oracular vessel like the *Foreshore*.

When a white-robed man and his blue macaw oracle turn a corner, the tall one, Lady Biota, once again grabs her fiancée's arm. "Doodle, oh! See the colors, such harmony!"

"Oh, I do! What a splendid creature! It would look well atop my new hat, don't you think?" says Lady Ouridia, gesturing upward.

"La," says Lady Biota, "very grand—if it did not topple you over!"

If it did not chew your pretty hat to shreds, Paseia thinks.

"But I am sure your little friend is perfectly lovely," adds Lady Ouridia, turning to Paseia.

"Small birds like Honor are best suited to matters of marriage and courtship," Paseia explains, lest their ladyships think either her or her oracle inferior, and then offers her customary line: "There is nothing less conducive to matrimony than a mocking cockatoo—we leave *them* for the politicians."

Lady Biota unleashes a hooting laugh. "Bless you, beautiful egg!"

Paseia obliges her with a smile, and then pauses at the correct door. She bows the women inside, her hand cupped against her chest. "Do have a seat, ladies."

The room is small, comfortable, and above all round. Three round, low-lying cushions encompass a round table, above which float two bowls of candied rose petals, one bowl of strawberries, and three glasses of ratafia. Several large, frosted glass spheres, lit from within, bob weightless beneath the ceiling's curve. A circular window affords them a view of the nebula, stars tossed among pink and golden clouds.

Once the supplicants finish arranging themselves on two of the cushions, Paseia seats herself upon the third. With poise, with grace—with an impossible insensibility to the ladies' dialogue—she takes the one object truly sitting *upon* the table, a wooden frame from which hang twelve small bells, and gives each of them an experimental ring.

Lady Biota plucks her ratafia from the air.

"Ah—by all means, my lady, but please mind your drinks," says Paseia.

"That means you, Beetle," teases Lady Ouridia. "I suppose we'll never find them empty."

"I do adore these small magics," sighs Lady Biota after a hearty sip.

"Certainly I cannot stop you from imbibing as much as you please," says Paseia. "I meant only that Honor might try to steal a taste."

"The dear! I'll not begrudge him," says Lady Biota.

"And then he'll die," says Lady Ouridia, "which signifies a charming start for our marriage."

Having unwrapped her scarf, Paseia dips her hand inside her loose collar. There he is: a little bundle of warmth beneath her clavicle. She pries his claws from her chemise and drags him, blinking, into the nebula's rosy light. The ladies' gasps gratify her. On-Your-Honor is a handsome fellow, soft as a peach, his yellow plumage fading to white and orange around his face. His eyes are bright as berries, dark as buttons. Still dazed from his nap, he stretches each wing separately, then shrugs both and shudders himself smooth. Paseia kisses his beak.

"I shall devour him whole," declares Lady Ouridia.

Lady Biota adds, "I shall smash him between my palms."

Paseia begins to like these women.

Lady Ouridia says, "I don't suppose we're showing the gods proper respect, are we?"

"Why should we, when they're tempting us with this delectable baby?"

"The gods accept any praise for their intercessors," says Paseia, her smile genuine. She finds it best to let the supplicants set the tone.

Honor gives them all a brief scolding before he turns an expectant look upon Paseia—"Yes, yes," she replies. Impatient he may be, but Honor is trained well enough that he waits for Paseia to offer him his treat: a strawberry from the floating bowl. He sets upon it immediately.

"Greedy thing," Lady Biota remarks.

"Simply voracious," Lady Ouridia echoes.

Paseia hates to interrupt their rhapsodies, but she must ask them the ritual questions. Her earlier joke elided the truth: all oracular visits are political, even the marriage blessings. Lady Biota, for instance, owns a textile manufacturing fleet, and Lady Ouridia's mother is expected to present her revised Silk Bill within the week. Paseia has done her research. The gods expect their interpreters to translate their messages correctly.

"My good ladies," she says, "we beg you attend. We beg you answer to your fullest ability; we beg you speak the truth." Phrased thus so that lies may remain unspoken. "We beg your patience as we proceed."

"I'm patient," says Lady Biota. "I don't know about her."

Lady Ouridia swats her fiancée's arm.

"Why," continues Paseia, "why do you, Lady Biota Leanax and Lady Ouridia Diphan, seek a holy audience on this day?"

"We can't very well do it after the wedding," says Lady Ouridia. "It's in two days, you know. Of course you are invited, and I don't mind telling you the party will be magnificent, for all that everything has been such short notice. Beetle and I were always going to marry—that is, when we were able, circumstances being what they were with Kadmos and his *exclusive* contract. Now that his and my divorce has gone through, how could Beets and I give up such an opportunity? Mumsy insisted we have a bird."

Only oracles can grant the immediate license to marry; without a consultation, partners must wait a month before they can be legally wed.

"I would be glad to join you," says Paseia, picturing herself at the wedding: tall and alone in her white interpreter's gown, a paragon of her office, deserving of the best but gently refusing to partake—but then, she must have *one* drink, so as not to offend her hosts. (Thanks ever so, you are far too kind, and yes, Honor *is* a splendid little gentleman, but don't let him hear you, he's proud enough already.) Though she'll be on a ship, still, she'll have the chance to taste a different air, tread a different floor. She will enjoy it while she can.

Visits off the *Foreshore* require an invitation—she'll have to get it in writing for the abbess—and then Honor will require a traveling cage, but those may be leased. Abbess Machaira welcomes her interpreters' reports of the outside; their consultations cannot be effective if they know nothing of the world.

Lady Biota gives Paseia her card, which will do nicely.

"And how long," says Paseia, giving thanks with a bow of her head, "how long do you intend this marriage to last?"

"As long as we can stand each other!"

"I cannot believe I agreed to ten years with Kadmos," sighs Lady Ouridia. "Five was quite enough for me! I think I shall keep *you* rather awhile, pet."

Honor volunteers either his agreement or his thanks for the fruit.

"Precious!"

"Perfect!"

"In what spirit," says Paseia, finally, "in what spirit will you, Lady Biota Leanax and Lady Ouridia Diphan, accept the gods' will?"

"Depends on their answer, doesn't it?" says Lady Ouridia.

"You think you're clever! We'll hear whatever the gods have to say to us," Lady Biota tells Paseia, her hand upon her partner's. "We have no fears."

Ignoring his objections, Paseia prizes the half-devoured strawberry from Honor's beak. "You'll have the rest soon," she tells him as she shifts him from her finger to the wooden frame.

No one but the interpreters can read the symbols etched upon each bell. Though the methods of divination differ for every oracle, the symbols remain constant. The star, the planet, the comet, and the moon; the sea, the shore, the wave, and the whirlpool; the seed, the shoot, the soil, and the fruit.

Honor dances along the frame, from one side to the other and back again, his beady-bright eyes fixed on the strawberry in Paseia's hand. She clucks at him, and he repeats the noise. Meanwhile the ladies settle into a hush, glancing at each other, at the bird, at the room, at the glorious nebula. Their fingers twine.

"What say the gods?" Paseia asks Honor and, at the unfortunate expense of the mood, adds: "Kiss kiss."

Lady Biota stifles a laugh.

Honor deliberates. He cranes his neck, settles his feathers, cleans his foot. Then, finally, he rattles his beak against one of the bells.

Paseia is too experienced an interpreter to frown.

"What say the gods, Honor? We must ask them several times," she explains to her supplicants. "Our intercessors do have wills of their own." She dangles the strawberry. "What say the gods?"

Delighted at her cheerful tone, Honor rings the very same bell. The wave.

"What say the gods?"

The wave.

Paseia breathes. Closes her eyes. Opens them. After rewarding Honor with the rest of his strawberry, she conjures a benevolent smile. "My dear Lady Biota," she says, "my dear Lady Ouridia. I am pleased to announce that the gods offer you their congratulations. Both they and I wish you a joyous union."

"There, now! Let the celebration begin!" Lady Biota clinks her glass against Lady Ouridia's and then, beckoning her to join in, against Paseia's.

"To your health," Paseia says, and draws a long sip of ratafia, ever undiminished.

***

"It was the wave. Every time, the wave. If he knew what it meant, I'd think he only wanted to annoy me. The wave!"

Abbess Machaira watches Paseia pace across her office.

"What do the gods mean by this?" she asks Honor, latched fast to her sleeve. "Why do we even keep the wave? Oh, I know we must say no on occasion, but nobody comes here *wanting* to hear it, do they?"

That rouses the abbess. "You did not tell them—?"

"I gave them the usual," says Paseia. Even with her friend the abbess, she must be more measured. "I tried to encourage him towards the sea, but I could not let their ladyships *notice*. Enough broadsides already accuse us of meddling."

The abbess remains seated at her reading stand, atop which perches her oracle, I-Beg-Your-Pardon. He is the abbess's third parrot, a cockatoo some sixty years old and, like his blind predecessor, in need of special care. To prevent him from plucking what feathers remain on his torso, he wears a sort of tight vest, whose knotted fasteners he chews while the abbess herself runs a finger down his neck. Her gloves are golden today, as is her veil; the fabric shimmers over her white hair.

"You want me to confirm that you did the right thing," the abbess says.

Yes—but she need not have been so plain about it, so *knowing*, as though Paseia once again wore a novice's braid. "I would not put you in that position, madam. The fault is mine. We interpreters must uphold our sworn duty. We must correctly communicate the gods' will."

"So long as their will is correct."

The stark truth of it almost hurts. Paseia collects Honor from her arm, kisses his head. He wriggles out of her hand.

"You are not the first interpreter whose oracle gave an unsatisfactory answer. Parrots are capricious beasts," continues the abbess, stroking Pardon's cracked beak. He leans into her hand. "As are the gods."

"What if their ladyships' marriage should fail? It would reflect poorly on our calling." And on Paseia in particular. Well can she imagine the caustic notes in the society journals, both her name and the *Foreshore*'s obscured or perhaps turned into a pun, but obvious nonetheless. She would receive no more wedding invitations, at the very least, and at worst—at worst she would be obliged to resign early. To give up the birds, her chance to train a macaw chick or soothe a cockatoo's last years. To give up Honor.

"Do you think their marriage will fail?" asks the abbess.

"Lady Ouridia and her husband did divorce early. And the wife before that—"

"Was but a year long agreement, and neither of those marriages received an oracle's blessing." She continues: "Do you think Lady Biota and Lady Ouridia will be unhappy?"

"No," admits Paseia. "They seem well-suited." Beetle and Doodle. Bless them, they're nearly the same person.

"Do you know of any other reason why they should not be married?"

"Not at present," Paseia says. "But may I conduct more research?"

Abbess Machaira's look is exasperated, fond. "You cannot recant your oracle's decision."

"I mean to reassure myself. That is all."

The abbess records a note and then, reaching into her skirt pocket, withdraws a heavy key. Freed and floating, it gently turns within a coil of silver ribbon, which Paseia ties around her wrist. Honor gives it a nibble.

***

Does Paseia believe in the gods? She pours the daily bowl of water for Kalliphrades, that Xe might bless her with clarity of thought. She lights the candles for Kalliphanotes and watches each one rise with its flame, that He might lift her spirits. She rings her bell for Kalliphronema, the patroness of oracles, that she might understand Her divine word. She murmurs prayers to all three of Them, that They might watch over the *Foreshore*, Their island in a galaxy so vast.

Islands, seas, oceans: Paseia has read about them. Oceans give rise to all manner of life. One day, if it please the gods, some grateful aristocrat will invite her to their planetside estate, and she'll see an ecosystem for herself. At least the library has pictures.

Paseia unlocks the *Foreshore*'s lone connection to the world outside. Each curving window is made of translucent glass, on which the library's catalogues are displayed; the stars' glitter backs the faint text. She unscrews the key, pockets its toothy lid, and with the inner stylus signs her name upon the glass. The text deepens in color.

She usually begins her visits with the *Beautiful Galaxy*, the journal least interested in scandal. She learns what the socialites are wearing, what planets they're visiting, what they're saying about the newest plays. (In her ten years as an interpreter, Paseia has been lucky enough to attend three.) Once she has an idea of how her supplicants want to see themselves, she turns to the more satirical publications.

Today she immediately brings up the new edition of *The Dowager's Eye*, in which Lady Biota is referred to as the next insect whom Lady Ouridia's mother means to collect.

The elder Lady Diphan is drawn as a giantess in all her bespoke glory: striped silk, layers of lace, and a hat double the height of her coiffure. Two silk moths flutter out of the open cage at her hip; a third silkworm perches upon her outstretched hand, which overflows with coins. "Milady Fripp woos her newest pets," reads Paseia. She enlarges the illustration and points to a flock of parrots entranced by the shine of Lady Diphan's treasure. "That's us, nugget!"

Honor attempts to steal her stylus.

Paseia tucks him between her chin and scarf, his favorite place. He curls into the warmth as she conducts a new search.

Ten years ago: *The Honorable Kadmos Gamet, proprietor of the Tropos planets, and Lady Ouridia Diphan, daughter of*

Parliament's Lady Diphan, sure in their affections, signed an exclusive marriage contract. Their friends at the Beautiful Galaxy *wish them their full ten years of wedded bliss....*

The Dowager's Eye, *two years ago:* Our sources tell us that a little bird—or perhaps a large one—has lately whispered in the Hon. G——'s ear; alas, unlike certain of his brethren, he heard nothing fortuitous about the coming Parliamentary session. We understand his temper quite shocked the innocent interpreter who merely relayed to him—and to us all—the gods' sacred word. The Hon. G—— was last seen at the previous week's masque unaccompanied by his wife, the incomparable Lady O——, who is said to have taken ill. We wonder whether her indisposition has aught to do with her lady mother's silks.

Paseia circles the date, then turns from the society columns to the *Chronicle's* archives: *Yesterday the Lady Diphan presented a bill before Parliament, in which she proposed that a higher tax be levied upon silk harvested from planets outside the Polukratid District. She claims that this will encourage production within the Polukratid's borders and so reinvigorate the Polukratians' stagnant economy....*

Apart from the usual innuendos about the interpreters' honesty, Paseia sees nothing relevant—which is to say, nothing that should concern her. That is how the abbess would put it: None of our concern. Let the aristos fight amongst themselves; if they want the legitimacy the gods' opinion brings, we will be pleased to accept their donations.

"What do you think, Honor? Does this sound like any scandal out of the common way? You're the one who said their ladyships shouldn't marry." She taps him between his closed and twitching eyes. "What are the gods trying to tell me, hm?"

He chirps, but it is only at the sound of her voice.

Does Paseia believe in the gods? Not more than anyone else. Does she believe that parrots alone can communicate Their will? Not particularly. But—she hesitates even to think such heresy, but she believes in the parrots themselves. She puts her faith in the strange spark of their brains: in their curiosity, their humor, their utter amoral confidence that the galaxy revolves around them. Truly, no other satellite enjoys its revolution so much as Paseia. It was for them that she became a novitiate at fifteen, for them that she joined Abbess Machaia's order. Perhaps they are not oracles, but she believes that these birds are special. If nothing else, the interpreters do good for the parrots, since their species no longer have any planet of their own. They are as alone as anybody else, suns unto themselves, and Paseia believes they deserve a place where they are nurtured, entertained, respected. Loved.

And she believes in being prepared. In this Paseia is not alone; her brethren are fastidious by nature. Many are the hours she's spent transcribing mageumaphone recordings, that no divine message should be lost.

She finds the transcript of Gamet's last visit, two years ago.

Interpreter: My good sir, we beg you attend. We beg you answer to your fullest ability. We beg you speak the truth. We beg your patience as we proceed.

Gamet: Suppose you can't rush the gods. Who's a good bird, then? [clucking noise] Who's a pretty parrot? Daresay the fellow could bite off my finger—well! [angry squawk] There's a lunge! Magnificent animal, quite the crest on him. There he goes again! [hiss] Pity about the shirt.

Interpreter: We do respectfully request, sir, that you allow the oracle to remain undisturbed while he deliberates; we should hate for you to receive a tainted message.

Gamet: Ah, the fellow likes me well enough—don't you, boy?

Parrot: [aggressive chatter]

Interpreter: Sir—

Gamet: As you say, ma'am, as you say. We'll leave him to it.

Interpreter: Why do you, the Honorable Kadmos Gamet, seek a holy audience on this day?

Gamet: She's got something up her frilly sleeve, doesn't she? Doodle's daft as a duck, and even she knows there's something wrong. The woman won't shut up about her Mumsy, and now that Parliament's about to convene it's 'I'm not hungry, dear' and 'I think I shall retire early, dear' and 'So sorry, dear, I already have an appointment with Beetle.' She won't tell me a [expletive] thing.

Interpreter: Your question concerns Lady Ouridia's mother?

Gamet: They're in it together, and Beetle too. Don't bother about her and Doodle being lovers—that's nothing to me—I mean the business end of it.

Interpreter: Might you rephrase your question, sir? I fear it is too imprecise for my oracle.

Gamet: Very well, ma'am, very well. The gods know my heart, but I suppose you can only do so much with a few carved blocks. How's this for you? I want to know whether dear old Mumsy's about to toss me out the airlock.

Interpreter: You are seeking reassurance that your arrangement with Lady Diphan remains intact.

Gamet: There! That wasn't so hard.

Interpreter: In what spirit will you, the Honorable Kadmos Gamet, accept the gods' will?

Gamet: She'd do well to remember I've got my own friends in Parliament.

Interpreter: You will hear the gods' will and act accordingly?

Gamet: I'll certainly take action.

Interpreter: What say the gods? [squawk; parrot footsteps; clatter] I see. What say the gods? [parrot footsteps; clatter] I ask again, what say the gods? [parrot footsteps; clatter]

Gamet: Now what does that mean?

Interpreter: [sighing] I am afraid, sir, that you will not like what I have to say. The wave here indicates that you—

Gamet: That [expletive]! I [expletive] knew it!

Interpreter: Sir, please—you will disturb the other supplicants—

Gamet: Let 'em be disturbed! Treacherous [expletive], that's what this is, an [expletive] con. I didn't [expletive] pay you for this [expletive]!

Interpreter: Sir, I must remind you that donations are voluntary. You did come to us for the gods' opinion—

Gamet: You're in league with her, aren't you?

Interpreter: The gods are impartial, sir. Even if they were not, I do not see how this would help Lady Diphan. She is, of course, free to come in supplication herself.

Gamet: The [expletive]! You [expletive]! All of you!

Parrot: [expletive, repeated]

Interpreter: I must ask you to leave, sir; you are upsetting my bird.

The transcription not unsurprisingly ends with the slamming of a door.

Pasiea is of a mind with the interpreter; it would be foolish of Lady Diphan to pay off an oracle only to tell Kadmos Gamet that she meant to betray him. Then, too, Gamet seemed to expect bad news. Why should he throw a fit when his suspicions were confirmed?—unless he secretly hoped for the opposite.

On her second reading, as she frowns at Gamet's behavior towards that poor bird (and gives Honor a swift crush beneath her chin), a certain detail catches her eye: the parrot was wearing a shirt. Several oracles are pluckers, but now Paseia recognizes this pair. The abbess herself conducted the session.

***

There is no more comforting sound than the raucous gossip of parrots at play, although Paseia's ears do ring after an hour or two inside the aviary. The paint is dimmed, the glass scratched, all the decorative nibs and knobbles gnawed. Here the birds climb the enormous gym, its perches built to suit every possible foot; here they destroy the week's offerings, bright blocks and lush tassels and floating wicker balls, so satisfying to crunch apart; here their interpreters learn their favorite toys so as to adapt these blocks or tassels or balls—or bells—into an oracular device.

Paseia joins Abbess Machaia upon her bench. Its knotty wooden arms stretch and spread into branches overhead; and Pardon trundles across them with that reptilian clumsiness particular to large birds. He ventures a croak when with a flash of wings he's joined by Honor, the smallest of acrobats.

"Clown," Paseia calls him, reaching upward. He disdains her finger. "Gremlin."

The abbess laughs as Pardon edges away from the tiny interloper. Then she turns to Paseia and lightly remarks, "You were a long while in the library, yesterday. There must have been new planetside pictures."

"Yes," Paseia says. It is reflexive, this need to smooth everybody's feathers. She breathes. "But I wasn't only looking at planets. I did find something, an old transcript from when Lady Ouridia's ex-husband...and you...."

After waiting in vain for Paseia to continue, the abbess shakes her head. "You can understand why Lady Ouridia divorced him."

"I think I do."

"Oh?"

The air thickens with laughter both avian and human. Paseia closes her eyes, opens them. Curls her fingers into her dress.

"Because of what he heard from the oracle, his people in Parliament killed the previous version of Lady Diphan's bill. She used that as an excuse to initiate divorce proceedings—and he was horrible to Lady Ouridia, besides—and then she encouraged Lady Biota's suit. Which," Paseia adds, with a society journal's self-conscious politesse, "I am sure has nothing to do with Lady Biota's planets and their fleet."

"Though I hate to belittle your efforts, this is common knowledge."

"In the outside world, perhaps."

"But you *have* reassured yourself," says the abbess. When no reply comes, she rests her hand on Paseia's elbow. "You care about your supplicants, that I understand. You want the best for them, but an interpreter and their oracle can only do so much. We are the gods' voice; theirs is the choice to act. The aristos' games shouldn't be any of your concern."

"With respect, madam," says Paseia, "they should not be any of yours, either."

During their long silence—oh, it stretches far too long—the abbess removes her hand and settles herself against the bench. A quarrel breaks out among several of the larger birds; they whirl heavily through the air and then return to their places as though nothing were amiss. They blink their lizard eyes at each other; they preen. As Pardon yanks at the fastenings on his vest, Honor dangles upside-down from a branch.

Finally: "What do you want me to say?"

Paseia's throat constricts. "I would not dictate your speech."

"Come, girl—you've made your elegant insinuations. Have the decency to back them up with plain speech."

Honor drops onto Paseia's head. "Hello, there," she murmurs.

The abbess waits.

"The donations," Paseia says. It is enough.

"Take a look around yourself," replies the abbess. "The gods are generous with their wisdom, but wisdom alone cannot keep a vessel in space. Wisdom alone cannot keep oracles in good health. Every day there are repairs, every day new toys. Every day there must be water, food—and that is just the parrots. Since you are so diligent a researcher, might I suggest that, instead of your pretty planets, you pull up the *Foreshore*'s accounts?"

"The planets I saw weren't so pretty." Her voice stings. "Too much of one crop ruins an ecosystem."

Take a look at them, she'd say. Just one look at the entire worlds given over to the trees on which the best silkworms feed. To cotton, to flax. Oceans sucked dry, forests uprooted, deserts watered, biodiversity become so much compost. How many hundreds of years, how many thousands until the planets recover, if ever? Or will Lady Diphan sweep in after a mere decade and terraform them anew?

And that, Paseia might say, is just the plants. Exploitation never stops there.

"Lady Diphan threw over Kadmos Gamet because she'd exhausted his properties," she continues. "And after this new bill, Lady Biota's are next."

"I see you're still wearing those Diphan silks," the abbess says.

"Were they part of Milady's bribe?"

Abbess Machaia's look lands on Paseia's cheek like a slap. Even for the abbess, that was too plain.

Everyone knows that the interpreters can nudge their oracles towards one answer or another. Everyone knows that the chance of a favorable answer increases with the amount of one's donation. Everyone knows. Nobody has proof.

With quiet fury the abbess stands, clucks: "Pardon, to me." He lumbers onto her shoulder. "Good boy."

Paseia clutches Honor until the abbess is gone. Then she lifts him face-to-face, looks into those eyes like shiny black seeds, and whispers: "What say the gods?"

***

One day later, the Lady Ouridia Diphan and the Lady Biota Leanax are married on the luxury vessel *Archipelago*.

By now Paseia has read so many society columns that she can almost write this one herself: *Lady Ouridia wore a magnificent sun-colored silk with a blue riband trim, and Lady Biota wore moonlight blue with yellow stripes. As the ceremony drew to its close, the elder Lady Diphan looked on from behind her golden spider-silk veil, where there were said to glimmer a few happy tears....*

If there were tears, Paseia wasn't close enough to see them. She stood at the base of the main dais with several dozen other 'esteemed guests,' including their ladyships' dressmakers, their milliners, their bakers, their decorators and their domestic magicians.

Thousands of floating, fireless candles illuminate the ballroom; their reflections outshine the stars. Though like everyone else Paseia dips her glass in the pool of champagne, she is too apprehensive to drink it. She can hardly believe she is here—but what could Abbess Machaia have done? She dared not refuse Lady Diphan's daughter the distinction of an oracle at her wedding. The ceremony itself blessed by the gods! And when Paseia returns, she will be obliged to make her report.

Already she sees that the wide skirts are thinning, and rather than bouquets of lace, hothouse orchids, almost violent in their color, decorate not only every column but half the socialites' hats. This season they're wearing feathers, too, and Paseia worries about their provenance; with any luck, they're from an ordinary molt.

Honor rides in a buoyant traveling cage, its slim chain affixed to Paseia's wrist. "Only a little longer," she tells him when he rattles his beak against the bars. "Oh, hush."

His loud objections draw the brides themselves.

"The dear animal!" cries Lady Ouridia.

"He seems even smaller than the last time I saw him," says Lady Biota. "I could snap him up!" She raises her hands, demonstrating.

"I often do," says Paseia.

While Lady Biota continues her chirping conversation with Honor, Lady Ouridia clasps Paseia's hand and thanks her for coming. "You do us a great honor—ha! That was an easy joke, wasn't it? But I am entirely in earnest. Beetle was so worried you know—"

"I was," croons Lady Biota, still at the bird.

"—Only I promised her that I would not let Mumsy come between us. She's my girl. Isn't that so, Beets?"

"I'm his now; sorry."

"Anything you need," says Lady Ouridia. Her fingers tighten around Paseia's. "You just ask us. Anything. Oh! Beetle, look, there's the person who did our hats. We must say hello!"

After Lady Biota gives Paseia a final, fragrant kiss on the cheek, she allows Lady Ouridia to drag her into the crowd.

"They're still aristos," Paseia reminds Honor.

Certain now that nobody is watching her, she removes herself to the ship's stargazing deck, where the merrymaking thins, where lovers stroll, where the tides of space stretch beyond sight. Where Paseia will meet a columnist from *The Dowager's Eye*, and at last put their insinuations into plain speech.

"This sort of thing," Paseia says to herself, rehearsing. "It simply will not do."

How easy it would have been, how natural, to imply that she expected a reward. With the money she could have leased a shuttle—perhaps even immediately, from the *Archipelago* itself—and left for one of the remaining natural preserves. She could have seen an ocean for herself, felt its spray on her cheek and its subtle roar in her bones. She could have smuggled Honor with her, a bundle of warmth between her chin and scarf.

Paseia could have and still can, but she won't. She'll return to the *Foreshore* and shudder beneath Abbess Machaia's cold eye. She'll stay and endure whatever punishment awaits her; she knows it will not be for long. If there are any further consequences—and there will be, the oracles and interpreters will suffer a blow—she'll have brought them on her own damned self, but she'll stay. Someone has to take care of the birds.

Heart Proof

Holly Schofield

Holly Schofield's short stories have appeared in Analog, Lightspeed, Escape Pod, and many other publications throughout the world. Find her at hollyschofield.wordpress.com.

Originally published in Wolfsinger's *Lightships and Sabers* anthology, April 2016

Kamik heaved the iron box onto the cart, her muscles aided by anger as well as decades of blacksmithing. Her next push centered its weight on the polished boards.

As she threw a rope over the box with more force than necessary, Techan appeared by her shoulder. "Let me give you a hand, old woman."

Behind him, the market square blazed unnaturally bright, silhouetting the bonfire dancers. Smoke drifted to the dark sky above where the god Welmit nibbled away the moon. The dancers would tire soon and the moon would return, allowing the villagers a few hours of sleep before the craftspeople's pilgrimage would begin.

"No need, old man." She ran rope through the cart's worn side slats.

Techan brushed a strip of birch bark off his shoulder and stretched out his gnarled, chisel-scarred fingers for the other end of the rope. "You could have affixed iron loops to the sides of the chest. Easier to tie it down." The iron chest was not designed to be transported but, among her completed pieces, the priest had deemed it her only sufficiently complex craftwork. The beaten iron side panels, the thick fire-proofing layer of fluffrock, and the heavy lid were almost more than Kamik's wooden cart could support. Loading it into the cart just so she could watch it burn in Welmit's Maw, the lava-filled mountain to the east, made it feel all the heavier.

"I could have done a lot of things," she said, yanking her knot tight.

As Kamik and Techan started to load the gear piled by the cottage doorway, their neighbor strode by, strips of birch bark wound tight in her hair. Markith's teeth gleamed in the firelight and she shouted well wishes across the darkness, making the cart horse stir in her traces. Kamik paused in her work only long enough to wave a hand.

Close on Markith's heels, the village priest trotted past, solemn as always. He glanced at the chest and gave the sign of blessing, crossing one wrist over the other, palms inward, then thumping his fists against his shoulders.

Kamik fiddled with a knot and pretended not to see.

Techan, of course, returned the blessing, holding the gesture until the priest was nothing but a narrow black shape against the bonfire. As a cough took him, his fists dropped and he clutched his stomach. The low hacking sounds carried over the reveling dancers' shouts. Like beetles consuming the heartwood of an ancient tree, Techan's cancers were eating him from the inside out.

Finally, he slowed and spit noisily. Kamik heaved a tool bag into the cart, barely glancing at the glossy black mass of blood that spattered across the iron band of the cart wheel and the toe of her boot. She kept her tone even. "I see I'll be taking your blood along the overroad, even if your stubborn self will be fighting marsh bugs."

Techan wiped his lips then snorted. "The overroad! You're really going to go that route, like a common merchant? Just to save two days of devout contemplation? Pah!"

"Welmit shouldn't care how a person gets there, as long as they throw away their life's work when they do," Kamik said, thumping a barrel of fresh water down beside the iron chest. "The overroad is perfectly all right to use, you old fool. The priest and his most devout followers—"

"The priest is an upstart, promoted beyond his abilities. And as for Welmit's devout followers having built it, *I* wasn't asked to help, was I?" Techan thumped a fist on the cart's sideboard, making the mare startle.

Despite her simmering anger, Kamik managed not to point out that only the young and healthy had been asked to cut down trees, move rocks, and apply the clever slurry that hardened and coated the new overroad. Techan didn't need a reminder of his age; just getting out of his cot in the morning was reminder enough of that.

"Just be glad I'm coming, old man." She moved away from him and slung her kit bag aboard. Unable to hold in her thoughts, she muttered below her breath. "Welmit's doctrines, senseless, destructive. Making us burn up treasures in his maw, doing no good for any one. Might as well throw in the village and all the people too."

Techan drew in his breath with a loud sniff. His ears must be better than she had thought. She could feel her face redden.

His voice was dangerously low. "You presume to say what Welmit should and shouldn't care about?" He uttered a short prayer, an apology to Welmit—as if it had been he that had blasphemed—and crossed his arms with hard shoulder thumps. "You presume too much, old woman."

Kamik gripped a sideboard. "Just be glad I'm willing to throw the fireproof chest into the only forge hotter than my own! It took me three years to perfect, as you well know! I'll be left with nothing but a drawing of my proudest creation and for what? A sacrifice to a god I no longer believe in!"

Techan stepped into the shadow of the cottage as two giggling pottery apprentices stumbled past, oblivious to their argument. "Hush, woman! The neighbors have big ears."

"And hard hearts," she said loudly, not caring who heard. She placed a foot on the running board and threw her bedding onto the seat. Lack of a sacrifice to Welmit required a person to leave the village, to travel "until the nuts and fruits themselves are unfamiliar" and to never return. The penalty was so severe, she had never known anyone to go against the doctrine.

She stepped down, turning toward him. The dangling birch bark entwined in his hair did nothing to soften the planes of his face. She touched his shoulder. "I'll do what I'm supposed to do, like I always have. Not for the priest, nor for you, old man. For Garva's sake, and the babe's. A child should have a grandmother." Their daughter's stomach had barely started to swell but Kamik had stayed up all last night making her a supply of herbal tonics for the days Kamik would be journeying. She had taken great pains to follow the exact recipe copied from the priest's scrolls, cooking the herbs in the small metal stove box that she had installed after the chimney fire.

Two steps took her to their cottage doorway where she grabbed a small crate from a stack of three. "This is my traveling food. I've packed you twelve days' worth," she said, her voice gruff, nodding at the remaining boxes. "Bring your cart around and we'll load it." Kamik had forbade herself to assist him that morning in loading his own sacrifice into his battered and ancient cart. The graceful wooden chair, which rocked at the touch of a finger, was light enough that offering to help pack it would have only wounded his pride.

"I don't need twelve days of food. Just six." Techan's voice was flat.

It took her a moment to manage the sharp tone he'd be expecting. "Not planning on coming back, is that what you're saying? Trying to shock me, are you, old man? Forty years together in this cottage, I know what you're thinking. And, you're wrong, you *will* come back and you'll be around long enough to see Garva birth her child."

She could not see his face in the dying light of the distant bonfire. It was a moment before he spoke. "I have already said the nine moon prayers for her babe."

Kamik set down the crate before it fell from her fingers. Saying the moon prayers in advance of the birth was against doctrine, against all tradition unless death was clearly inevitable. Techan really did believe his cancers would send him upward to the endless sun. Had he been hiding his stomach pain more than she knew? Or was he just disheartened at the way growing older ground a person down like spices in a pestle?

For a long moment she busied herself placing the food crate in the storage area below the cart's seat before swinging back down onto the rutted road. One foot slipped and she landed on her bad knee. She stayed in the welcome shadow of the cart for a moment before rising, crouching in the bitter-smelling mud that had grown slick with strips of birch bark.

There was nothing Kamik wanted more than to have this pilgrimage over and done, and both of them back safe. However, despite an early start each morning of the four-day journey, despite not stopping at any villages along the way, she was not the first to arrive at Welmit's Maw. Markith had forced her horse and cart past Kamik on the last stretch of the overroad, where the forests gave way to open grassland followed by bare rock. The fierce eagerness on Markith's face as she had passed, eagerness to toss her river raft with the clever deerhide floatbags into the inferno, made her normally pleasant face look insane.

Kamik had long since stopped looking back over her shoulder. Behind her, a long line of carts stretched, full of all the other mad and driven folk.

Techan was not among them.

Of all the village craftspeople, only Techan had chosen the more traditional route along the underroad. It would be two more days before Kamik could expect him to arrive at the Maw. Kamik's heart, which Techan once described as clad in the strongest iron, ached more than her swollen knee. She should have gone on the underroad, foolish as it might be.

"Give me a hand, neighbor?" The shout from ahead demanded a response. Markith had already reined in at the largest of the open, smoking lava pits and unstrapped her raft. Her voice rasped like Techan's after long hours in a smoky workshop. Kamik should have crafted her an iron stove too but, in the past few years, she had not found the time, spending every spare moment on the fireproof chest.

There was scarcely room to squeeze between Markith's raft and cart bench. The woman must have slept uncomfortably on the narrow bench the whole journey.

A push from them both and the raft slid on its wobbly leather underbags through the cart's open gate. Kamik scarcely had time to notice the tiny careful stitching on the bags before the raft sunk into the fuming depths of the pit. The molten rock seethed, mirroring the colors of the late afternoon sun.

Kamik reluctantly echoed Markith's crossed-arm blessing before clambered down off the woman's cart onto the shiny black rock that ringed the smoking crater.

"Welmit renews all!" Markith's wrinkles creased in a smile as she climbed back onto her cart bench and slapped the reins. Her horse pulled the cart forward on the path between the open pits. Words drifted back over her shoulder: "Your turn, Kamik."

Her turn. Her turn to throw years of work into the fires of one of Welmit's many maws. It had hurt three summers ago, the last time Welmit had eaten the moon, when she had tossed in a wrought iron lantern and it would hurt more now.

"Hurry up, then!" A young apprentice, one of old Perga the weaver's boys, held his horse's reins and gestured impatiently at the pit. Behind, others climbed down from their carts.

"Give me a minute. I'm in contemplation. Have you no respect for doctrine?" Kamik frowned at the boy.

Doctrine.

She slowly loosened one rope that held the chest fast.

Doctrine had made her take this pilgrimage.

Doctrine said the fireproof chest she had worked on so long should be consumed by Welmit's greed.

Anger filled her.

Why should an ancient destructive tradition, probably developed by a priest who had never lifted a brush nor carved a stick in his life, dictate what she should do?

When would she become old enough to outgrow this childish custom?

Why did Techan willingly undergo such needless suffering?

Her horse shifted uneasily in its harness. The shouts behind her grew louder as the queue of villagers grew more impatient. Welmit would bring bad fortune to the entire village if any one of them failed to burn their offerings before sunset of the day of arrival.

"Kamik, elder. Why do you delay? Do you not want to feel the ecstasy that comes from sacrifice?" She had not seen the priest approach. He spoke mildly but with narrowed eyes.

"I'm sorry, Priest, forgive me."

"Only Welmit can forgive, elder. And he will be grateful for this sacrifice. If this chest can protect our written doctrines from fire, then the improved chests you build in ensuing years will please him as well. Your offering is both clever and worshipful."

"Thank you, priest."

"However, I'm sure you don't want to deny the others their turn. It will be evening soon." The priest's face grew sly. "And you don't want to miss seeing the tiny face of your new grandchild, I assume?"

Kamik clenched a fist behind her back. She cast around for excuses. "I must wait, Priest. I must wait for Techan to arrive so we can experience the ecstasy together. It will be his last chance to do so."

She almost bared her teeth in grim pleasure when the priest hesitated. She had finally shut the man up.

He raised a finger. "I...I would have to pray on it but I do believe it may not satisfy our living god, our sacred god, Welmit. Such an action, however kind it may seem, is not necessary according to the doctrines.

"It is necessary to *me*. In fact, I must go find him." She climbed into her cart. A slap of the reins and her mare broke into a brisk trot.

The priest's shouted prayer for her soul and for the village fortunes grew faint behind her. She kept up the harsh commands until the mare was almost at a gallop and the cart was swaying, until the fork in the road was in sight.

She pulled the reins. "Whoa."

If she turned left, this path would loop back to the overroad with its fast dry track, and she could be warm in her cottage in just four days. She might never see Techan again but that was Welmit's way, creating people who lived solitary lives, even those that shared a cottage. She had heard that there were lands where it was different, where people led their lives as a couple, compromising at every turn, but such a practice seemed hard to fathom. There were no reasons, no doctrine, no promises that required her to turn to the right, down the unkempt underroad toward Techan. He would not expect her to do so. The pitted underroad, treacherous in the growing darkness, threaded between open lava pits, pits no longer used for sacrifices due to their propensity to cave in at the edges.

She glanced back at the smoke-filled landscape behind her. Beside the queue, the priest was looking her way, one hand on his brow to shield the setting sun. She crossed her arms as if in prayer and mumbled a short apology to Garva and the unborn babe before ostentatiously thumping her shoulders. The mare whinnied in surprise when she yanked the reins, forcing the cart to the right, to the underroad.

As the moon rose, the mare picked her way, slowly, steadily. Kamik's head began to nod. Sleep had been scarce the last four days.

A jerk broke Kamik's gentle doze. The mare avoided some brambles, leading the cart over a particularly stony stretch. A faint glow from the ground ahead decided the matter and Kamik called a soft "whoa". A quick exploration revealed a bubbling, steaming spring next to a small lava pit. It would give her hot water for her dirty face, maybe even a bath.

She pushed aside some stunted birches exposing the pit further, a concave opening agleam with hot red coals. Molten lava, crimson and black, flowed down one side, disappearing into a crack. The pit was old, abandoned. The lava must have resurged out this vent just today—a sign of Welmit's wrath with her. No, she shook her head, still half-asleep. This was simple good fortune. Perhaps she could heat up her supper too.

An idea occurred to her and she sketched it idly in her mind. If she could make the chest smaller, the size of a flask, she could keep her dinner hot for hours. A fine idea that would take some tinkering to work. A wave of homesickness swept over her. Oh, to be in her workshop, pumping the bellows at her forge, pounding iron on her anvil until sparks flew. The things she could invent!

The fireproof chest was only the beginning. She pictured the drawings she had left behind. All the details of how she had beaten the side panels to the perfect thickness—tough enough to withstand most cottage fires. How she had found the right combination of coal and size of forge to make the fluffrock expand and pop like corn kernels. She had drawn the diagrams on fine deerskin and left them on the hearth at home, as if challenging Welmit to burn them while she was gone. It had only been a few years since her careless housekeeping had caused the fire that had consumed all of her and Techan's lifetime of records. Now, it seemed almost as if another person had lived that life. Another person had built that chest.

A new thought struck her: here at this tiny pit, she could give the iron chest the ultimate fireproofing test. The cart held a small shovel, useful for wheels stuck in the mud. That and the water bucket should do.

She approached the smoking pit, shifted her feet to a firmer footing, paused as yet another thought struck her, and began to scoop the almost molten rock.

***

It was not until late in the third day along the underroad that she found him, where a widening marsh had softened the road. Techan's cart lay tipped at the road edge, the broken wooden axle raw and white against a large moss-covered boulder.

She rushed forward. Why had she not crafted him an iron axle? Why hadn't she strengthened the iron bands that wrapped the wheels?

Techan's horse raised its head from where it was hobbled in a drier patch that was still more reeds than grass. Where was the old fool?

"I'm over here, woman." The voice was weak but—Kamik was relieved to hear—sounded irritated.

He lay at the edge of the marsh on a pile of wet leaves. He had apparently gathered wood some time ago but not managed to light a fire.

"Techan. Are you hurt, my one?"

He looked startled and she realized she had not used that particular endearment for several years. She touched his weathered hand.

He began to answer but coughing wracked his thin cheeks. The food crates she had packed for him all those days ago lay nearby, looking almost untouched.

"There was no point in you coming," he finally managed to say. "I will not complete the pilgrimage."

"Shush," she answered, as if he were a child. She began to gather fir boughs, chopping off the springy green branches with her hand axe.

By sundown, she had made him a comfortable bed and cobbled together a broth from dried deer meat and herbs.

The fire crackled, sending sparks up into the darkness. Techan managed to swallow a few spoonfuls of broth before he set the bowl aside.

"Are you well enough to sit up, old man?"

"There is no point in tending to me, I keep telling you. I will not make it to Welmit's Maw. I may as well close my eyes here and not open them. To have promised that chair to Welmit,"— he gestured at his tipped cart—"and not sacrificed it, it's blasphemy. I will die a blasphemer." He closed his eyes to drive the point home.

"Silly old fool."

Kamik re-hitched her mare and backed her cart across the sodden uneven ground until the rear end was steps from where Techan lay. She snuck a look and was pleased to see the firelight reflecting in his watching eyes.

She walked over to Techan's ruined cart and rescued the rocking chair. The seat back—carved into an image of Welmit's many fiery mouths—caught the firelight.

Techan had closed his eyes again.

"It's fine, not even a crack," she said. "You can stop pretending you're not looking."

"Taking the chair yourself to Welmit's Maw does not cease to make me a blasphemer. I must witness the sacrifice. Did you forget that, old woman?"

"Fortune favors you, old man." Kamik set the chair carefully on a clump of marsh grass next to her cart.

Techan cracked open an eye.

She used a stout branch to pry open the fireproof chest. The lid lifted then crumbled. Smoke and heat surrounded her and she fell back, coughing hard. After a moment, eyes streaming, she was able to see the coals she had shoveled in were still fiery hot.

A river of lava cut a channel as she watched, oozing like scarlet mud. Sure enough, the chest had held the temperature steady.

She could not hide the pride in her voice. "There is nothing in the priest's doctrines that prevents Welmit's Maw, or a few buckets of it, coming to you, old man, is there? That should be just as worshipful as you visiting the Maw."

Techan tilted his head to one side, as he considered her words.

Kamik sat on the fallen log she had pulled close. Side by side, they watched the lava cool, swirling into patterns of red and black, much as they had watched the fire in their hearth every evening all those years.

"Woman?"

"Yes, dear one?"

"Do you know why Welmit wants the sacrifices? Why he designed such a practice?"

Kamik threw a twig on the fire in disgust. "Your last few words, and you want to waste it by explaining doctrine to me? Do you know me at all?"

Techan continued as if she hadn't spoken, "Why did you make the chest?"

"Because I wanted to protect all of our diagrams, since I can't protect the craftwork itself from Welmit's greed, his complete and total avarice." It felt good to have somewhere to direct her anger.

"Why did you want to protect the diagrams?" His voice was as patient as the stars overhead.

Kamik practically sputtered. "The waste, you old fool, the waste, burning all the good craftwork we create!"

"If you could have kept the chest, would you have made the diagrams? If there were no sacrifices to Welmit, would your mother have been as diligent in teaching you the blacksmithing arts? Would you have been as diligent in teaching Garva? Would Markith have taught her sons to make those clever boats?" His voice was thin but sure.

Kamik sat straighter.

"Perhaps not," she conceded after a moment, rubbing her knee. Could Techan be right? Would every minute detail of the village's craft knowledge and artistry be completely communicated to other generations if not for Welmit's demands? Would the younger villagers have created such a clean fast road surface if the trip to the Maw had not been necessary?

Techan rose up on one elbow. "Don't believe in Welmit's powers, old woman. But do believe in Welmit's results. They work." Coughing wracked him. "Take an apprentice, pass on the knowledge, record what you can and keep it in many marvelous chests like this one. Maybe even burn an offering or two." More coughing. "No matter where you end up."

Techan lay back, his energy spent.

A crooked glowing line appeared along the left seam of the chest. It, too, was at the end of its natural lifespan.

He was right. Without sacrifices to Welmit, the village would not have so many marvelous things. They would live in mud and squalor, dying young, like people did in other lands. The offerings were an essential part of a complex, deliberately repetitive system that passed on knowledge from one villager to the next, from one generation to the next.

Kamik rose and held the rocking chair in her strong blacksmith's hands. With snapping sounds like splintering bones, she broke it into several pieces, the chair that Techan had shortened his life for, the chair that Garva would never use to rock her babe to sleep.

Piece by piece, she fed the bits of chair into the smoking contents of the fireproof chest. Techan watched closely, his face slack but his eyes bright until the last piece was consumed.

Later, much later, as she held Techan's body in her lap waiting for the dawn, she realized a new village, a new start so far away that the trees themselves were unfamiliar, meant the chest's design would now travel much further than the nearby villages—banishment was yet another way to keep the new knowledge secure.

Welmit—or whoever had designed the doctrines—had thought of everything. She slowly raised one fist and thumped it against her shoulder.

C-a-l-l-a-s

Katharine Coldiron

Katharine Coldiron's work has appeared
in Ms., the Rumpus, Theaker's Quarterly
Fiction, Kzine, and elsewhere. She lives
in California and blogs at the Fictator
(fictator.blogspot.com).

Solomon had heard opera for the first time two months ago, in a terrible audioshop out in the cluttered misery of Oxon Hill, a ramshackle dwelling with filthy 'phones. His standards for audioshops had declined precipitously in only ten months, as he chased and chased after more and more music. The sound quality in that shop was totally inadequate, full of scratches and the background speech of long-dead bootleggers.

But the randomizer had gifted him with a heavenly sound: three men singing, in turns, bouncing from voice to voice, a devastating melody. Their voices were obviously more trained, more uniquely skilled, than any he'd ever heard, and they sang in one of the dead languages, a European one Solomon didn't recognize. Later he learned it was Italian, that the name of the piece was *Don Giovanni*, and that the scene was about a descent into hell, a deserved penalty for sins unnumbered. That this form of music was called opera, and that the State considered it the most dangerous form of banned vocal activity.

The experience was staggering – the emotions that washed over him while he listened, and the instant desire to hear more. He revisited every audioshop he'd tried, searching "opera" in every redband archive he sat down to, allowing the search to envelop his life and his income even further. He asked the shop runners about opera, he asked fellow patrons about it (all of which was against the unwritten, unspoken rules of audioshops). Hastily spelled words took him to snatches of recordings: *Lucia, Figaro, Tosca*. He learned terms: tenor, aria, vibrato. He kept searching, kept asking questions, kept finding moment after moment of ecstasy in the stolen minutes when his eyes would roll back and his neck would slacken, just in listening, just in hearing. And one word kept making its way to the surface of his fevered inquiries: Callas.

Callas was a soprano from the middle of the 20th century, 200 years before the bacteria and the inception of the State. Her career was short, but her legend seemed unmatched. Fellow audioshoppers had read about her, had heard tell of her from third parties, but no one he met had ever heard her. She was not to be found in the archives. Solomon pursued her, asking more and more questions, less and less cautiously. Where could he hear Callas? What songs had Callas sung, and which were the best ones? He spied on the selections of other shoppers and struck up conversations with anyone he noticed listening to opera. Many of them had never heard of her.

Finally, Bicky, the proprietor of the greasy Oxon Hill audioshop where he'd first heard opera, had given him Capone's name and set up a meeting. Since history was all the citizens of the State had after music and film had been forbidden, it shouldn't have surprised Solomon that a street thug knew of a criminal as quaint as Alphonse Capone, but it did. Solomon had asked for a date a few weeks distant, to give him a chance to change his mind, and he spent that time trying very seriously to stop desiring music. He failed. And so, tonight, he waited for Capone at 14th Street and H, running his thumb over the smooth button that ejected his fingerboard from his sleeve. He wouldn't use it at all that night, he'd decided. ISL only. Much safer that way.

Throughout this quest, Solomon felt increasingly as if he was the object of some shadowy scrutiny, as if something was chasing him even as he chased opera. Nothing he could put a finger on, like anonymous types following him down the street or glancing away from his eyes on the Metro. Just a general uneasiness. His doorbot using a voicebox to mention how late he was coming home, instead of signing to him. His boss asking why he rushed off after work every afternoon; had he met someone? Even his bank taking a few extra microseconds to process transactions on his home display. As if it was all being recorded for someone else's ears and eyes. All along he had hardly used his fingerboard, cautious about monitoring bugs, but there were other ways to track him.

Perhaps he'd been reckless. The love of opera had consumed him, and he cared about little else aside from hearing more. Callas was his Holy Grail, and as he drew closer to her, he found more and more dissonant the structure of life under the State.

Fourteenth Street was still more or less deserted, and the next security sweep was a few minutes away. Solomon decided to duck into a small electronics store on the corner until the bots had passed by. Inside, he fiddled with a coffee table/display surface idly, spinning stock pictures in place, caroming framed videos off each other with small flicking motions. The surface was cruder in texture than he was accustomed to, even for home tech.

One of the videos was the Secretary-General's latest mouthpiece, whose voice Solomon quite liked. Sonorous and toffee-textured on the ear, he was a big improvement on the screeching girl of three years ago, who, despite her position, hadn't seemed used to the idea of speaking at all. Some of the other officials' mouthpieces were nice, too, but the Secretary-General often had the best of the bunch, since he had to deliver more precious words than any other speechmaker. With mild curiosity regarding this week's pap, Solomon selected the video and unmuted it.

"...continue to strike at the heart of our union," the mouthpiece was saying. Since he'd started visiting audioshops, Solomon secretly wished that, just once, a mouthpiece on vid would break into a song of some kind, any kind. Of course, no one bred to be a mouthpiece would ever have done something so subversive, so it was a foolish desire, but it gave Solomon glee to imagine it. "We shall have to strike harder and faster than they if we wish to maintain our way of life. Starting next spring I will roll out a series of new measures intended to stamp out all subversive elements that threaten the State, from peddlers of dangerous cultural flotsam to purveyors ah– uk–"

The mouthpiece was making froglike sounds, jutting his chin and jaw forward as if choking on something. He put one hand to his throat and another to the podium, to support him as his body tipped forward.

"Is he hacking up a lung?" came flatly from Solomon's right elbow. It was the speech of a fingerboard. A cheap one, by the sound of it, uninflected and metallic. Solomon did not respond. He was watching the vid, as the Secretary-General's mouthpiece struggled.

"Ock," he said. "Ock. Ock. Ock." As if vomiting.

"He's lost it," said the fingerboard to his right. "His voice is gone."

At almost the same moment, as if the mouthpiece, speaking in a studio somewhere in Central, had heard Solomon's companion all the way from 14th Street, he ceased convulsing and stood straight and smoothed the front of his plain black shirt. *I am finished*, he signed. *I'm sorry, Jenny.* A security bot materialized next to the mouthpiece and escorted him away.

A young woman with a terrified expression accentuated by her slightly protruding eyes walked to the podium. She stood there a moment, and then opened her mouth. "I am...Secretary-General Carlos Al-Amin," she said, a faint squeak on the second syllable forgotten by the camel's-hair softness of the tenth. "Starting next spring, I will roll out a series of new measures intended to stamp out all subversive elements that threaten the State..."

"I've never seen that," said Solomon's disembodied neighbor. "Never seen a voice expire on vid before. Have you?"

Solomon turned to address his loquacious friend briskly (his fingers were poised to sign "leave me alone") and found himself facing a short man, plump with wealth, wearing an absurd old-fashioned suit, two-toned shoes, and a weirdly sexy hat that Solomon believed was called a fedora. The dude grinned with half his mouth, and his fingerboard said "Guess not."

You Capone? Solomon signed.

Let's go in the back, the man replied in kind. He took Solomon's elbow and hustled him behind the counter of the store, which was old enough to have been designed with staff in mind. Through a door, through a dim, grimy stockroom, and then the squat man held out an arm for Solomon to step into what looked like a tiny bomb shelter, a concrete box that could comfortably hold about 1.5 people. He stepped inside, and the man followed. A stark light from the ceiling illuminated the box as soon as the door closed (with a frighteningly permanent sort of sound).

I'm Capone, signed the squat man. The smell of a virile cologne was very strong in the small space. *You're Solomon, right?*

Right, signed Solomon, something relaxing in his chest. He had half believed this was a setup, that the idea of meeting a fellow named Capone to find opera was the entry to a trap.

What're you looking for? Bicky didn't tell me much.

C-a-l-l-a-s, signed Solomon.

Capone did nothing for a moment, looking at his garish shoes. *That's serious shit*, he signed at last. *No joke finding it.*

But you know where to find it, right?

Capone hesitated again. *Can I show you something else?*

C-a-l-l-a-s, Solomon spelled again, recalcitrant.

Sure, Capone replied. *I got you. I just think I got something else that might turn your crank.*

What is it?

You'll have to wait and see, said the little man with a sidelong smile. *What do you say? You got the funds for a little field trip?*

Solomon had brought cash with him that he thought was sufficient for Callas, so he nodded.

Two thousand? Capone persisted.

He nodded again. Small change.

Let's go on the town, then, signed Capone.

***

The two men took a bicycle rickshaw from 14th Street, for which Capone apologized with the tinny voice from his fingerboard. He had drivers, he explained, but he thought it would be better all around to stay anonymous on this one. Solomon wondered if Bicky knew more about Solomon's job, family, life than he'd thought, and if Bicky had passed on that information. The cyclist pulling the rickshaw looked Tajiki, maybe, but anyway didn't seem the type to answer anyone's nosy questions about her route that night. Solomon fingered the eroding velvet of the seat under the shadow of his thigh. They glided several blocks in silence.

A high-projected vid became visible between buildings: the mouthpiece, choking on his own dead larynx. Unlike Capone, Solomon had seen it before. In a restaurant. A woman kneeling, asking the woman in the opposite chair to marry her for then and always. Her voice, the only one, rang through the room. She got through the proposal, got through the happy acceptance and the tears, and her voice broke and ended mid-syllable when she tried to tell her new fiancé she loved her. The fiancé paled, grew stricken, as the woman coughed flatly.

Even before Solomon had become obsessed with music, he had had a perverse interest in the world before the bacteria. He had read as much of the literature as he could get his hands on, which, with his clearance at The Agency– its business so secret it didn't have a distinguishing name– was plenty more than the general population could. A lot of it seemed fragmentary, as if it was a puzzle that had been jigsawed and then shoved back together with half of its pieces discarded. There was an astonishing amount of conversation, in any case. People seemed to chatter endlessly in these records, using their voices for the most trivial things. They talked on telephones, they talked (or shouted!) at parties, they talked with their mouths full. A ceaseless ribbon of conversation from birth to death. Solomon knew they had no idea how precious a commodity a voice could be, having mostly not had to do without. But still. Didn't they realize how wasteful it was to expend such a resource on words that mattered so little?

Capone prodded the rickshaw cyclist in the back. She nodded and hit the brakes.

They had traveled southeast, to an even shabbier neighborhood than before. Some of the architecture on 14th Street and H had been converted to billbuildings whose screens were now dark or snowy, no longer advertising the latest tonics and gadgets. Here, the conversion hadn't even taken place. The buildings were blank stone or brick, their textures rough and strange. The streetlights had a sick orange cast. Capone and Solomon disembarked and it took ninety seconds of Capone standing still and gazing across the street at nothing before the penny dropped and Solomon pulled out his wallet to pay the cyclist, who pedaled off directly.

All right, come on, signed Capone. He cocked his head in a slick gesture and walked off. Solomon followed. They went about a block and a half, and then Capone turned down a narrow driveway between buildings. His two-tone shoes crunched against pebbles on cracked, wet pavement. Solomon began to fear more than slightly for his safety; there was really nobody around, just dogs barking here and there (they lost their voices much more quickly than cats) and the strange muddy dark of the backyard Capone was leading him into. It must have been a sort of small preserve at one time, with a curving path created by splotched, discolored paving stones, once a manmade stream leading to a little pool. The overgrowth all around was sagged with this afternoon's rain. The empty pool was wracked with weeds and there was a nest of some kind in its corner. Rats, likely.

The house that abutted this little ruin was boarded up and decaying. The fence to the west of the property had missing planks and Capone was already crawling through it. Solomon followed. A terrible shack had been erected in the neighboring yard. Warm light shone through gaps in the boards and dark smoke drifted from a steel cylinder on the roof. There was a potent chemical smell.

Capone rapped on the shack's door, which leaned, hinge-free, on the structure. He ejected his fingerboard and said "Lenore!"

Something stirred within. The door tilted open and a woman emerged. She had layered bags under her eyes and hair that expressed utter surrender to frizziness. She wore a shapeless nylon garment without sleeves. It may have had a prior life as a tent.

She carried an early-model fingerboard, a clumsy thing without a wrist harness. It even boasted a delay between her birdlike typing and its alien speech. "Why'd you bring someone here, Capone? Why didn't you call me to come there?"

"He's not here for the usual," said Capone. "He's a Muesli customer."

Muesli? Solomon signed.

They aren't programmed with the word m-u-s-i-c, the woman signed to him with furious fingers, then typed again. "I won't do that work anymore."

"Just this once," said Capone, with a slimy wheedling expression that would have convinced Solomon to do exactly nothing.

"Just this once until the next time."

"No way. He really wants something special, is all. I promise he's the last one."

Lenore sighed, dropped her head, pushed her hand into the tangled pelt of her hair. "All right," she said.

She said. With her own voice. Solomon nearly took a physical step back, it surprised him so.

She lifted her chin and opened her mouth.

Hush, little baby, don't say a word,
Mama's gonna catch you a mockingbird.
When that mockingbird don't sing,
Mama's gonna buy you a brand new thing.
Hush, little baby, don't say a word,
Mama's gonna catch you a mockingbird.

It was her own voice, and it was singing. Right there outside the pile of shabby boards she lived in, here in the murk of southeastern DC. Solomon heard her with his own ears.

A tear slid down her face. Her voice was a cracked, broken thing. The song barely resembled anything Solomon had heard in the audioshops over the past year. If every song he'd yet heard was a flag in the wind, hers was the torn and muddied banner of a lost battle.

"That was terrible," said the dead whine of Capone's fingerboard. Its synthesis was even more unbearable against the real vibrancy of Lenore's real voice, sad as it had been. "Really lousy."

She dropped her fingerboard on the ground and signed frantically. *I did what you asked. I want my money.*

"Why should I pay you for that? I brought him for Muesli, not garbage."

Please, she signed. *Please.* And again and again. *Please. Please.*

"I gotta go," he said. "Get a new dress, okay? You should be ashamed." He began to walk away, and she grasped his arm, below the elbow, her eyes flashing with need. He shook her off and headed for the open fence.

Lenore put her face in her hands and seemed to shrink. "Oh," she gasped, one more word.

Solomon fingered the obscene wad of cash in his pocket and looked at the frizzy halo of her hair, trembling as she wept. He cleared his throat and swallowed some saliva. She was taking no notice of him and Capone was gone. He'd never been so aware of the fineness of the fabric that covered his body.

He extracted a hundred from his pocket, came closer to her, and placed his hand on her thin shoulder. He could feel her bones, thin and brittle like a sparrow's. She lifted her head, her expression clearly anticipating a blow. He pressed the bill against her hand and she took it with a small whiffed breath.

"Thank you," he said, with his voice.

She met his eyes for another moment, and then her face crumpled and she brought her hands, cash and all, up to her sobbing again.

There seemed nothing else for Solomon here, so he removed his hand from her shoulder and took a cautious step away. He did not look back after he went through the fence.

"I'm really sorry about that," Capone said from his fingerboard right away when Solomon had caught up. "She was raised to be a mouthpiece. In a clean farm somewhere. They tossed her when they caught her singing to her baby." He shrugged. "I wouldn't have thrown out a sweet deal like that."

Babies born in families like Solomon's, where money wasn't a desperate topic, were hushed to silence upon their first babbles and shipped off to certified clean nurseries. The bacteria had somehow been flushed out and kept out of those facilities, and some people were born, lived, and died in them, taking vows of vocal preservation to raise innocents far from the worst areas of concentration. Depending on their aptitudes, these children were groomed for various vocations. They were taught ISL and how to use a fingerboard before they could hold a stylus, the better to preserve their voices for what mattered, whatever it turned out to be. Solomon himself had shown few talents aside from his poker face, so he'd been shunted into intelligence programming.

If he'd had a winning smile and a talent for acting, he might have been chosen as a mouthpiece, at which time his voice would have officially belonged to the State. Just as Lenore's had, if Capone had her story right. Singing was a bad enough crime, Solomon knew. Singing for herself, or for the enjoyment of a creature from whom she could reap no profit, was a violation calling down the scorched-earth life Lenore had obviously lived since then.

Solomon considered the potential shape and texture of such a life for a moment, and was silent.

Then he again signed C-a-l-l-a-s.

"Look," said Capone. "I know I let you down on this one. I thought Lenore could do better than that. Last time she did a lot better."

Solomon was already signing, trying to interrupt. *It doesn't matter how well she can s-i-n-g a regular s-o-n-g*, he said. *That isn't the point. She's not an o-p-e-r-a s-i-n-g-e-r. No one is. I want audio. I want C-a-l-l-a-s.*

Capone sighed. "You're really breaking my balls, man."

Solomon kept his hands folded.

C-a-l-l-a-s? signed Capone.

Yes.

How about next week?

How about NOW?

"Shit, man," said Capone's fingerboard. "No need to lose our tempers. I know Lenore was a bummer, but…"

C-a-l-l-a-s.

"Right." Another sigh. "Okay." He pulled out a tiny smartpad, the size of a business card. His fingers flew over it for a moment. "You go to this address. Flash the back of this at the front door. Show this page—" he let Solomon see a crude, pixelated smiley face with eyes that rolled like a sick dog's "—at the VIP room, and tell them what you want."

He handed Solomon the minipad. *Will they have—*

"You'll see when you get there," Capone smirked.

Solomon read the address – a posh corner very far from here – and swiped over the screen to make sure he could call up the scornful smiley. He turned the pad to look at the back, and saw a red fingerprint embossed in the polymer. *What do I owe you?*

"Finder's fee is five thousand," said Capone, his eyes steady on Solomon's. He was aiming much higher than he expected to get, Solomon intuited. "They'll probably charge you twice that for what you want."

Lenore, signed Solomon. *And my trouble. You could have saved me half an hour if you'd just given me this* – he waved the minipad – *back in Northeast.*

"Four thousand," said Capone. There was sweat on his upper lip.

Thirty-five hundred.

A long moment, in which Solomon wondered if the little man had it in him to murder Solomon right here in this ruined back-yard and take his entire store of cash. He guessed yes, but that Capone was calculating the hassle of such a move as opposed to how much Solomon probably had on him.

I have to get more cash uptown, too, added Solomon. *It's a hassle to go so far into Central this late at night, and I live out of town.* There wasn't a grain of truth in any of this.

"Thirty-five hundred," Capone repeated, after another tense pause.

Solomon nodded and reached into his chest pocket, where fifteen thousand-note bills were stowed. He peeled out three, handed them to Capone, and took five hundreds from his pants pocket.

"For my trouble?" Capone said, smiling like a crocodile.

Solomon took out his wallet and threw a tenner at the little man. It fluttered to the antique paving stones, and Solomon walked away as Capone dived after it.

***

It was after one when he arrived at the Slow Club, which was the building that corresponded to the address on the minipad. The signage for the club was minimal, just twelve-inch white cursive letters a few feet above street level. There was no one outside. No bouncer-bot. No windows. Solomon fidgeted with the smooth net of his pocket lining.

Feeling silly, he knocked on the door, or what he assumed was the door. It was a door-sized black slab situated on the diagonal corner of the building, but it seemed impenetrable aside from its four edges.

A circular area at eye level shifted and transmuted until a processor bot was gazing back at Solomon. A *very* high-end processor bot, the kind Solomon was not yet experienced or trusted enough to write code for at The Agency.

Solomon fumbled the minipad out of his jacket and held up its reverse to the transparent oval in the door. The processor bot emitted a tiny red light and the fingerprint on the back of the minipad glowed slightly in response. The bot did not acknowledge Solomon, and its oval faded back to sheer black. In just a moment more, a series of servo noises sounded around the edge of the door, and then it opened and a brief but powerful vacuum drew Solomon inside the Slow Club.

The first thing there was to notice was music. Song. The quality was fuzzy, the recording old, but that somehow added to its charm. A man was singing, his thin, reedy voice floating over the untidy mutter of expensively modulated fingerboards.

Someday, when I'm awfully low

And the world is cold

I will feel a glow just thinking of you

And the way you look tonight

The lighting was so dim that Solomon couldn't see much detail, only the sense that he was surrounded by murmuring gray statues. He looked around as casually as he could. People were passing *books* back and forth, to his astonishment; real paper books.

And strange shiny disks, too, of what purpose Solomon did not know. Nearly everyone had a beverage.

There was a small sign on the opposite wall: VIP □. He went that way, shouldering suits and dresses with scents that tantalized and textures he could have happily smothered in. He looked at chins, so as not to be rude enough to recognize anyone.

Presently, he faced another impassive black wall. No transparency materialized after a moment, so he swiped to the leering cartoon face on the minipad and held it up next to his own. The door dissolved in amoebalike patches, revealing a black booth with a chair and a vid display. Solomon entered and sat. The door reassembled itself and Solomon had the sensation of swift movement, as if the room was an elevator.

The display activated itself and a very pretty Uncanny appeared. She smiled. "What can I do for you tonight?" she asked.

Solomon hesitated. Despite his parents, his high-security job, all the societal perks he'd had access to – and despite his crawl through every seedy audioshop in the greater Washington area over the past year – he had never been anywhere like the Slow Club, so redolent of money and secrecy in equal parts. He feared he would be outed as a fraud any moment, that it was all an elaborate trap.

But he was here. He had a pile of cash. He had come so far into forbidden territory, had fitted the last of his savings into two pockets, had tangled with Capone. It was now or never, this or nothing.

C-a-l-l-a-s, he signed at the vid.

The Uncanny smiled some more during a few seconds of

processing time, and then she said, "I have one record for that request. Would you like to experience it?"

One record, thought Solomon, *damn*. Callas had been so famous in her day that he'd expected to be able to choose from a selection of recordings.

Still. This or nothing. He indulged himself with one more moment of dithering, and then signed *Yes*.

"Please insert twelve thousand seven hundred notes."

Dear God. He hoped the door charge for the Slow Club wouldn't be more than he could pay. He slipped the cash into a square depression that had formed in the table, where it vanished.

The Uncanny smiled a little more broadly. "Please enjoy your selection."

The vid faded to black, and white words appeared. *Verdi. Otello. Piangea cantando. Maria Callas, 1963. Nicola Rescigno.* The lights eased down. Solomon lifted his hand, but could hardly make out its lines, or the dark button below the root of his pinky finger, by the light of the white letters on the display. Then the screen faded and all was blackness.

He waited for a minute, two, three. No 'phones appeared. He had just begun to wonder whether something had gone wrong – the word "trap" flitted into his mind once more – when it began.

The music emitted from all around him, as if the black booth was itself a set of 'phones. After barely twenty seconds of instruments– Solomon still hadn't memorized which were the reeds and which were the strings– the voice began. It lifted quickly into song, made itself known, speared Solomon to his seat, and then emitted so soft and quiet a phrase that he leaned forward to hear it better. Later, he would realize that this was one of the clearest recordings he'd ever heard, but at the moment he was so urgently listening that his breath came in miniature sips.

The voice lamented. Wept. It repeated a word over and over, in threes: "sull-chay," or something like it. Italian again. At times, drawing out "sull" so long and so quiet that it seemed a whisper, fearful or shy or both. The word could have meant anything. Its actual meaning was irrelevant, since the sound communicated everything the listener needed to know.

The voice rose and fell, expanding in glory and retreating in sorrow. It cried for everything, for every sin and injury in the history of the universe. It was the most beautiful thing Solomon had ever known.

No other opera compared to this. Nothing on earth compared to this.

By the end, when the voice pierced the sky in a vibrating note that seemed to last a week, his face was streaked with tears and he was gasping as quietly as he could (to hear, oh, every single note). It had seemed over, before that note, and then, after more of the instruments, it seemed like it wasn't finished.

But it was. The lights lifted gently and the Uncanny appeared on the vid again. "I hope this experience met with your satisfaction," she said, her simulated voice a corpse twitching with electricity next to what he'd just heard. "Would you like another selection?"

Again, was on the tips of his fingers. But he couldn't afford it, most practically, even aside from the problem of sincerely wanting to do nothing but listen to Callas until he starved to death in this little black box. He couldn't gather the wherewithal to reply properly in ISL, so, without thinking, he pressed the button that ejected his fingerboard. "Just give me a moment," he managed, his voice, too, a dundering parody of a human sound.

"Take as long as you need," soothed the Uncanny. "I am available when you wish another service."

***

The voice danced above and around his thoughts, shimmering like a trembling lamp. He kept hearing that last high note, the way it shone out in a ray, slicing into his heart, a shock that raised every single follicle of hair on his body.

He had staggered out of the Slow Club without looking up much from the muffling carpet. A voice at the door had gently urged him to come again, but he had not had to pay any more. He had concentrated most intently on not listening to the music burbling over all else in the club so he wouldn't lose every nuance of Callas.

But it slipped away even as he flogged his mind to repeat it. The melody was leaving him, the exact shape and color of the notes. Ephemeral, momentary: the only thing that remained was the strong sense that more Callas would save his life, just as continuing to subsist without Callas would end it.

There was no more Callas. Solomon tried to wrap his mind around it. He did not have twelve thousand notes to spend every week to keep himself sane.

Maybe I should just... He thought of the GW Bridge, the ugly gutter of hardpack that ran below it. He thought of the pistols on the belts of security bots, easily grabbed for one fatal moment. He thought of turning himself in for his treachery, asking for swift justice against a subversive such as himself.

He glanced at the street signs. He'd been walking for half an hour, tormenting himself with the fading miracle in his head, not trusting himself enough for the Metro or a taxi. Nearly home.

Nearly home. I'll sleep on it and see if it looks different in the morning. It's just one voice, and there are plenty of audioshops. Lots of songs yet to hear.

Just one voice.

Solomon thought again of Lenore, of the broken wing of her song. Doubtful that the paltry sum he'd given her would do much good, but it might have meant one night she could have stayed in without answering when Capone knocked for her with a customer.

Then self-pity washed him again. He'd taken measures to preserve his voice for 24 years, hoping to say something once that mattered. No one could predict how much could be had from one voice, whether you'd lose it after three sentences or a lifetime of soliloquy. You could predict certain things; in the thickest urban forests, New York, Chicago, DC, you'd surely be able to say less. The warfare, the bacteria, had been concentrated there, hadn't cleared so successfully as it had done over the Great Plains and its flat horizons. The less said about Los Angeles– where the bacteria clung to the drapery of smog and feasted heartily on vocal cords with every last breath– the better. But in general, every person was different, every life a different possibility. Solomon didn't want to take any risks. He wanted to get married, say "I do," tell his children he loved them. But now it all seemed so pathetic, so pointless. When voices like Callas's had existed in a world before the bacteria, why save his paltry words for a day that might never come?

Forgoing the elevator, he trudged up four flights of stairs. Why indulge in elevators? The world was dying anyway. He took a moment to roll his eyes at his own melodrama before thumbing open the door to his apartment.

Solomon dropped the roll of remaining bills in the bowl by the door and hunched over the hall table, peering in a mirror at his own eyes. Dark circles ringed them. The relentless chase of music had drained him of so much – money, energy, good reputation – and it had been a year, now, since the start of this thing.

"Now what?" he said aloud. He dared to laugh, a short, ugly bark.

The recessed lighting over the sofa came to life, illuminating a slim man sitting in the living room with his legs crossed. He was clad in black and had a handsome, forgettable face. Solomon startled backward and knocked over the bowl by the door. The wad of bills bounced out and came to rest in plain view of the man on the sofa.

Unremarkable as he was, Solomon recognized him. He was greeted at The Agency by Solomon's superiors with broad goodwill, a hum of fear underneath. He brought in more violators than any other tracker in the District. *Just give me a moment*, Solomon thought with a sickening thud. Only five words on his fingerboard, but enough to smoke him out, to trace his path.

"Mr. Solomon," the man's fingerboard said, and he smiled pleasantly. "You've had an interesting evening, I trust?"

The Last Shaper at The Witch City's Waypoint

Emily Lundgren

Emily Lundgren is a student of fiction at
the Northeast Ohio MFA and a Clarion
UCSD 2017 graduate. Her work can
also be found in Shimmer Magazine.
When not writing, she is probably
lighting the bonfire at The Dreg Heap
in Dark Souls 3.

Ess sang he found me in the reeds in the heat of summer, my mother a crow lying dead.

I was too young to know my first shape. He sang I pissed and shit and cried all the time, and he thought more than once about leaving me for the bears to raise. But the bears are all dead, which I didn't learn until I was old enough to hunt on my own. *There is another world*, Ess used to sing, *between the paths of these ruin-woods, kept from us—and that's where you come from, little kit. The shrinelands, the black hills, the old warrens. This is the curse you inherited from your mother: to live out your days in the bones of the lost witch city Gea, to keep the books, as I did.* But then Ess was gone—taught me there are no shrinelands the same way there are no bears.

Taught me how the wind prowls and pines for you if you dare to get lost in the pathways.

***

Then: Roo, my sister. Her disappearance happens in the spring; she turns the wrong corner under the shadows of the black spires and disappears, eaten by the wind. That's how I imagine it happens. Sometimes the paths will play tricks, north turns south, could be east, might be west, but Roo could always find our way. I search for her as careful as I can, for days, for three moons, taking care not to get lost, taking care to mind all the corners of the ruins. Then by the river that cuts the heart of the crumbling spires, too afraid to get lost, too afraid to search all the places I've never been, afraid of the wind that might undo me—on a hot afternoon in late summer, I stop on the steps of a crooked path and I let myself cry. Ess found Roo in the winter after my tenth summer, young and scared, wolf fur as white as the snow and paws cut with ice between each of her toes. She wouldn't speak. Never spoke. But she was kind, she was clever. She was brave. And then I'm done, and she's gone, and so I stop looking. I rarely leave my den.

***

Until Ess, our singing had no written language, so he taught me the languages of books instead, called common, and a scrap amount of a language he called witcher—the yarns and a handful of crude phrases, most of them akin to *fuck the bitch queen* and *would you like to suck my big prick?*, and *I am guilty of nothing* and *yes, that is a gutty challenge, pretty boy* and *I will eat you to spare your mistress a sorry rut.* He didn't like conversing it aloud. But before he lost himself—he showed me letters he created for our words, and he put a feather in my hand, and he told me to write all his songs about our great patrons during the time of the Raven as he sang them, and I was so glad to do this, so awed by his wits to find symbols in our singing, I didn't hear their sorrow until long after he disappeared. They're the only thing left to remember him by.

One begins: In a time before time, something attacked something else, and there was life.

***

I go hunting, but I make traps, something about the thrill of a catch less rewarding without Roo. The common weasel struggles, the snare caught around its chest and neck chewing deeper through its skin. When it catches sight of me, it pants little squeaks, its eyes bulging. Blood stains the breeze from the strangle of wire. I shape human, take off the curve of sharpened antler from the leather string I use to carry it around my neck. I coo, "Thank you, goodbye." Catch it by the throat, dig the sharp of the antler hard until it spasms. I work undoing the snare. Undo the wire, reset the catch. I wipe the antler in the grass, place it around my neck against the sling of worn leather where my map fits snug. But when I'm about to shape, I stop, going still.

***

There! she appears through the seam of a telling, on the breeze. From a different path of direction, no easy one. A woman, like Roo. She wades through the tall grass. Makes pleading sounds at me like she'd been looking for me all this time, trips until she is only crawling. Decorated strange. Far, far away on some other string of paths, there's a nest of angry howls and cries rising above the ruin-woods—cut short, like the slamming of a gate. She comes so close, hand outstretched as if to touch me. My instincts catch. I startle, shape fox. Her eyes widen before they roll back into her head. She goes limp. Ratshit on this afternoon, for leaving my den.

***

Ess sang once, just before he disappeared, that he heard voices hiding in the eaves of trees, in the shimmer of the pines. The fabric of this place is thin, he'd sing, the magic is dying. Then Roo drew once she saw a man running, not me, on the deer paths, skidding out of sight, unwound by the wind. I thought they were batshit. This woman is far from Ess and she is not Roo—I take the weasel from my trap and I mean to leave her, but then she's awake, and she's making strange sounds and going on and on and rubbing at her eyes. Her hair is the shortest I've ever seen, half of it down to the scalp, the rest a mess of curls, the color pale, blond—speckled by blood. I can smell it. She smells all wrong, like rust and a tangle of other things I can't place, like scabs and rot, maybe. I think she might kill me and I should hide, but fear stabs me in place.

The woman digs in a pocket of her strange decoration. Boots, shirt, pants, a whole outfit I wouldn't know what to make of, only Ess would collect things like that from the ruins. Forgotten things, clothing, cups, toys, coins, bottles, buttons. The books usually told him what they were, what they meant or used to be—what to make of them even though he couldn't read very many. They're forgotten, too, as forgotten as most of their languages—the many not in Ess's common.

But then she's pinning something shiny to her collar, fixing a button inside her ear, and then like it's no trouble at all, like she's grown up beside me, the two of us—she's singing like a shaper, out of breath, pointing at me. "Don't you dare rutting move, dog-man," she sings. "I think my ankle's sprained—ratshit!" She heaves in a great breath, painful, cursing. "Ratshit!"

I drop the weasel out of surprise and I shape human. "Don't rutting move?" I sing to her.

"Knew it," she sings, but it's seething, through teeth. "Now, really! I have seen some real batshit catshit in my day—ancient sea slugs, the insides of a world-eater, I've even seen a man *turned into* a toad—but I've never—*ever* seen a man turn into a dog, then *back* into a man." She shakes her head. "But that's the universe for you, infinite and full of dogshit—hey, you going to help me, or just sit there gawking like *I'm* the one that's been running around the woods naked?"

"Help you," I sing, "eh, why would I do that?" I eye her, wary. "I'm not stupid," I sing.

She meets my hard look, then pulls off something from her belt, and points it at me. I frown, unsure what it is, other than colored black and red, and maybe dangerous by the way she aims between my eyes. "For dogshit sake," she squawks, "it's a gun! Nevermind the make or model, since it doesn't look like you've got less of a clue what plasma, lasers, or *bullets* mean—"

"I'm not stupid," I sing.

"I heard about that."

I shake my head. "Eh, you're batshit if you think I—"

She laughs mean, takes aim and shoots behind us, into a crumbling archway of ruin. I duck with a whine, covering my ears. The sound scares me more than the light that explodes the rock in a plume of dust and smell of something burning. "Basically," she sings, "it does that, only it does it to your guts—it turns smart guys like you inside-out. Now—I *order you* to *never again* call me batshit, help me up, and take me to like, I don't know—your *place*, in this shithole. Then water, seeing as I doubt you've got a commlite hooked up to the Interstellar Military Alliance. We might be stuck with each other, come to think of it—but we'll figure it out. Draw a line in the dirt or something... I haven't got anything to steal, so—don't even think about it."

I scratch up behind my ear, confused. "You're not from the shrinelands, are you?" I sing.

She sighs. "No," she chirps, "I'm from up there." She points up at the blue cloudless sky.

***

The woman tells me to call her Shar. I don't tell her what to call me until she prods about it and waves her gun around. Then Kit, I sing, and tell her my shape is not a dog, but she doesn't listen. Instead she remarks on the curliness of my hair, how tall I am, my tan skin in contrast to her bloody *pallor* as she called it, then moves on to observing the narrowness of alleyways, the strange obsidian ruins, the spires on the horizon. I quickly learn she is nothing like Roo because she will not shut up. I'm used like a crutch, ordered to stay human—until it turns out her ankle isn't sprained, and I'm glad to let her go—her smell isn't what I imagined the sky might smell like. Bloody, like a hunt. Then, by the time I think I should've led her off a cliff, or led her into a trap, if I were Roo, smarter—I've led her straight to Ess's den, the folds of damp earth, of books.

I light the lanterns, since there's no natural light. Try to keep my back from her, until I can't when I spark the hearth—I'm wound, all tense, knowing she's watching, still afraid she might kill me, but not as afraid of her as I am of the gnawing wind lurking around the wrong corners. I have the fleeting thought she could be a witch, unable to explain her any other way, and I turn, fully expecting her to have her gun raised, still pointed in warning. But it's not, and she stands with a furrowed brow in concentration, eyeing the shelves, the stacks, the table, scrolls of parchments, crow feathers, ink pots. She whistles a babble of nonsense, not song.

Then without asking, she picks up the nearest book on a stack near the door and fingers through it, briefly, before letting it go for another, her gun tucked at her belt. My frown turns into a glare. I bawk at her. "Those are mine—be careful, they're old, aren't they, eh, can't you tell—"

"I can't read any of these," she sings, like she's troubled by it, like she should be able to. "I mean, they're all in different languages, aren't they?" She crosses the den and sinks into my best chair facing the hearth. "Now I'm starting to get a little spooked, Kit." She winces, rubs her shoulder. "Exactly what's this place of yours doing with a shithole full of dead languages, eh?"

"They're not all dead," I sing, "I know common, I know witcher. I know shaper, too—"

I fetch her one of the books in common, showing her and taking the chair Roo used to curl up in every winter, nose to bushy tail. Shar lingers on it, seems to become even more troubled. She must read several pages before she speaks, and it comes out in a low song, a flinch. "This is Mandarin. It's dead, too—or it has been, for a long time. I should know, my parents were some of the last who knew it. But they're gone..." There's a pause between both of us, and I think maybe about Ess, about telling her—but then she's moving on, giving me back the book and forces it out of me, anyway: "Exactly where are the rest of your dog people these days, Kit?"

"Okay," I sing, "I'm not a dog, also, eh, they are gone, they got lost, the wind ate them."

"Dog, fox, wolf, whatever," she chirps, "none of you were actually born here, were you?"

I scratch behind my ear, off-put. "Ess sang no, but Ess might've lied. I don't know—"

"Eh, but what's the *last thing* you remember, in the other place, then? Before this one?"

"*Eh*, maybe don't interrupt me," I bawk, glaring. "I was singing I don't know because it happened when I was only a pup, if it happened at all. It didn't happen to Roo until later, but she couldn't sing anymore, and she was still a pup, too. Then Ess. Ess *never* sang about it. He called this place a witch city, witch ruins, witch curse. He hated witches. He sang they warred with us, they locked him up and threw away the key. He sang we are all from the shrinelands. But maybe, maybe he would've sang anything to us—how would we ever know any different—understand?"

Shar rubs at her eyes. "Rutting ratshit," she whispers, tipping her head down, covering her face. There's a great shudder that moves through her, a breath gathered, maybe the edge of a sob before she calms. I wonder if I imagined it. "This is a tear," she mourns, "It's a waypoint..."

"Eh?" I prod, anxious because of the way she sings it, because of her face, grown grim.

"The last thing I remember, I was on Roi, way out in Andromeda, no joke. You know, we've been at war in that rutting galaxy since the moment we showed up, that's the truth, and I've seen it all. I know I don't look it, but I'm getting on, Kit, like two-thousand-something—centuries kind of melt together. But anyway, I was on Roi, running my rutting rump off from a bunch of rutting— uh, *vampires*, I guess, is the best thing to call them—one even used to be my rutting girlfriend, the whole thing sucked. So I tried to phaze to my starship, but I must've tripped something or, ratshit—I don't know. It felt like one of them ripped my leg off—I had this gut of pain. Then I ended up here. Exactly what," she sings, "do you make of a song like mine?"

My skin crawls, a sensation so human I startle, breath catching. I don't understand half of Shar's story but I hear the sorrow, the undercurrent in her tune like every song I sang after Roo disappeared. I blink, scratching up behind my ears. I try very hard to understand what Roo might've understood. I try hard to think of an answer, a clever one, the right one... But I can't, and so Shar goes on. Goes on and on with more songs. Songs that come from the sky and stars.

She describes pockets of worlds inside constellations, torn by wars that have lasted ages, ripping the universe at the seams, creating cracks in reality that you can sometimes slip into if your death isn't careful enough. If it isn't clean. "I don't understand," I chip at her, shaking my head until my chirping turns to growls, until I go back to calling her batshit, crazy in common, lunatic in witcher and worse, because singing isn't as cruel. She only watches, until I'm finished.

Then she prods: "Look, haven't you ever heard of ghosts? *Spirits?* You've lived a ghost life here, Kit. You died. Long ago, maybe the moment you were born..." and that's it. That's when I tell her she has to go. I tell her I hope she gets lost in corners, that I hope the winds eat her away. "The winds!" she laughs at me. "I've been eaten by worse. By space worms and moon wolves, bellies full of iridescent planktons, the prettiest most delicate things you've ever seen. I'm not afraid of being eaten by the wind—no rutting way. Don't you worry, Kit, I plan to get as lost I can here, and really—if you're *actually* as smart as you sing you are, you'll do the same..."

***

But what does she know of anything, this woman from the sky?

It's dark by the time she leaves, and I track her, troubled, wary of her songs, her bravery.

I watch her while shaped fox, from the farthest edge I dare go as she disappears under the black shadows of the spires, under the spread of infinity—thinking about Ess, about Roo, about my fear coiled like a ball of snakes underneath my fur. I asked her, before she left the den, I sang: then what will happen, if it's true, what will happen after you are eaten—what's on the other side of the corners, what will happen if the wind blows backwards? But Shar just shrugged, and stretched her arms, heading for the dug-out door. "The great mystery," she sang, "maybe it's different for all of us. Maybe you'll find your shrinelands, and maybe I'll find my parents. I like imagining something sweet and gentle, worth the long journey. But really, it's anyone's guess."

**

My favorite book holds a song of a warrior who is visited by a fox-spirit. Eventually, they fall in love and leave the warrior's world for hers. They become partners of the sky. In most witcher yarns the foxes are always tricksters—they lie, or steal, or run away with treasure or hearts of men. But this one is different. There's no depiction of bloody war, there's no dead mothers or fathers, but still it unfolds like soft rains split by the sun. I take it with me when I leave my den, following the scents of Shar, the worn leather of her boots, the dried tang of blood. I trot down the familiar ruin-paths, conjuring up Roo's smarts and Shar's bravery. I follow the dusty deer trails leading into the roots of the black spires. I carry the book in my sling, hoping that when I greet the wind, I have something to sing to it. Something kind, and glad, and good.

Adjuva

Arkady Martine

Arkady Martine is a speculative fiction writer and, as Dr. AnnaLinden Weller, a historian of the Byzantine Empire and an apprentice city planner. Under both names she writes about border politics, rhetoric, propaganda, and the edges of the world. Arkady grew up in New York City and, after some time in Turkey, Canada, and Sweden, lives in Baltimore with her wife, the author Vivian Shaw. Find her online at arkadymartine.net or on Twitter as @ArkadyMartine.

Wandering creates the desert.
- Edmond Jabès

Michel dreams the dead at Antioch again.

They rise unbidden by any word but God's, with their wounds
still gaping, each one weeping as if it were a saint's reliquary.
They still have their weapons. The sand stirred up by the living feet of what remains of their army drifts through them on
the wind, leaks out their eyes and haloes them with a grace that
Michel can barely remember. The walls of the citadel are merci-
lessly high, impossible to scale without ladder and rope, and still
blistering with the sun-wizened faces and glittering spears of the
Turks. The dead do not care. The dead care only for the crusade,
for God and His Will. They die a thousand times over again.
They are inexorable, an untimely and uncalled-for resurrection,
and Michel cannot remember enough of the shape of *deus lo volt*
to fill his mouth with, stumbles on *deus adjuva* instead, instinc-
tive, remembered, *God aid us*, help us, help *me* —

He wakes up parched, his mouth full of desert dust, spilling out
the corners of lips too chapped to bleed.

He spits.

It doesn't in the slightest help.

Outside, it is raining, sheets of droplets puckering the surface of the Bosporus. There is no way save providence or deviltry that Michel is still alive; by the looks of the city beyond the window it is the year of our Lord two-thousand-something-with-sky-scrapers, approximately enough, and he remembers being a man already thirty when first the pilgrim knights came into the desert that is Jerusalem.

Thomas is sitting crosslegged on the windowseat. Despite the steaming of his cup of tea, he has not moved an inch in the night. He is like Michel's very own personal gargoyle, except less inclined to keep foul spirits away.

"Entreaties hardly ever work," Thomas says, and inhales the tea-steam. It fogs up his glasses and smells of bergamot all the way across the room.

Michel rolls over in the bed and considers shoving his head underneath the pillows and ceasing to breathe. "And you would know this how?" he asks.

"Long experience," says Thomas. "As well as trial and error."

Michel inhales air through his nose, tasting the luxury of humidity. "Mostly error, from over here."

"You're the one who keeps asking for help," Thomas says, arch, and then sighs. His teacup rattles in its saucer. "I just want to get things right. Where are we this time?"

"Istanbul," Michel says. "Again. Look out the window, you idiot."

Thomas puts the tea down. "Sorry," he says. The Golden Horn curves itself peaceably enough outside the glass behind him.

The tops of the new construction in Taksim glitter in the rain. "I was watching you destroy the sheets."

"Perverse."

"Sympathetic. Sacked or not sacked?"

"What, the sheets?"

"Constantinople. You're deliberately obtuse."

"Istanbul. So, yes, sacked, but not currently. Looks perfectly fine from here, nothing falling apart I can see, up with the AK Parti —"

Thomas flicks tea droplets at him from his fingertips. He never burns himself, which is the least of the ways he is infuriating. "Do shut up," he says. "It's a crossroads, Istanbul."

"It's the center of the goddamn world, Thomas. Which is why we keep ending up here. That, and it being the most direct route from Europe to the Outremer —"

Thomas interrupts him. "You can't call it the *Outremer* any longer, not if we're in the twenty-first century this go-round, it's gauche. As well as orientalist."

"Kindly spare me from the idea that you've spent the night reading critical theorists. I wasn't aware that you could get that bored."

"It isn't as if you were here to keep me company. You went to Antioch all alone."

"And woke us up in the twenty-first century, apparently. In which you can make use of all that postmodernism."

"Critical theory is not boring," Thomas protests. He seems more concerned with this than with how he and Michel have arrived again at the beginning of the crusade, the entire journey undone again.

Michel struggles up on his elbows. "Thomas," he says. "Are you *capable* of boredom?"

"Nearly a millennium, and I'm still here with you. What do you think?"

The rain that drips down the windows casts rippling shadows on the ceiling over the bed. The frame of Thomas' glasses glints like feldspar in the dimness, and Michel cannot quite make out his expression.

"Let me sleep?" Michel asks.

"You'll dream."

"I'm *dead*."

"Hardly makes a difference."

***

This is how an army starves itself: there are not enough villages between Anatolia and anywhere else to glut ten thousand pilgrims on, even if each one did not come with his very own sword and the promise of heaven if only he could figure out what to stick it into. In another life, Michel tells himself, he will understand supply lines. This is not supposition but fact. In another life, he does.

Marching dissolves the boiled leather of his boots and bakes the hair on his head bone-white. His ribs have enormous swooping hollows underneath them. There is salt caked at the corners of his eyes and he does not remember crying, or having enough moisture inside himself to cry. Marching also translates him from this world to a finer one, remakes him and each of his companions in fire, and if marching takes them through a Hell borne from the plains of Megiddo, so be it, if it brings them at last to the gates of a heavenly Jerusalem rather than to the earthly one –

"You're being self-indulgent again," says Thomas.

"Oh fuck *you*," Michel says. He turns around, spreads his arms wide like wings. "Look at me. I've been dragging my ass from Constantinople to Jerusalem for eight months –"

"Eight centuries. You'd think we'd learn."

"Well, forgive me if I'd like to get there once in my miserable existence."

Thomas pokes him, delicately, on the shoulder. His fingers are skinny and go right through Michel's shirt, which is sapphire blue and polyester-cotton blend, and thus an abomination to the Lord but not to GQ Magazine. "Mortification of the flesh?"

"This is my dream. If I want to walk through an apocalypse, I will."

"Accidental apocalypse," Thomas mutters. "When Alexios Komnenos asked us to show up he just wanted a bunch of mercenaries."

The road they're on is going to be Highway O-21 whenever the government in Ankara gets around to building a connection between Aksaray and Tarsus. Right now it's paved and that's all that can be said for it. The sun reflects up off the asphalt.

"Let's leave the Byzantines out of it. We're not here for them. *I* went on this trip because of the sermon at Claremont."

Thomas laughs at him. "Whoever shall determine upon this

holy pilgrimage and shall make his vow to God, offering himself to Him as a living sacrifice, holy, acceptable: he shall wear the sign of the cross of the Lord on his forehead or on his breast?"

"Urban was good at what he did," Michel protests, without much rancor.

"Too bad he didn't want to come along."

"Why, Thomas," says Michel. When he's got Thomas staring at him through the lenses of his glasses, he crosses himself, grins, gestures toward the bleached-blue desert Heaven that shines down on them both. "Of course I'm not on Crusade. There's not sufficient penance in this world or the next to save *my* soul from Hell."

Thomas, gratifyingly, flinches.

***

Michel is inside the citadel.

The infidel is *outside*.

This recent reversal of fortunes would not be quite as funny as he currently finds it if the selfsame infidel did not have a sufficient supply of food, an item which Michel, along with all the ragged forces of Bohemond and Raymond d'San-Guilles, entirely lacks. They have starved Antioch into submission; they have taken the city four days prior, with the help of a lie and an army of the dead given back to them by the Lord, and here within this citadel they shall starve, sundazzled and besieged, surrounded by Turks and madmen.

There's an army risen from the barren sand outside the walls, as if someone had planted dragon's teeth in the dust. Turks are all that would grow here. There's no water for anything else.

Thomas – Thomas *proper*, Thomas as Michel first met him, resplendent in a dusty bloodstained tunic and matted hair, the light of blind fervor and nothing else in his grey eyes, gets down on his knees next to Michel and says, "God is testing our resolve." He makes the sign of the cross. He is facing Jerusalem. In this first moment he lacks everything that Michel will learn about him in the centuries to come: despair, and cleverness, and the inhumanity of either a devil or a saint.

This is a terrible dream. It is never over.

Michel is surrounded by madmen. Perhaps he is also mad. If the Crusade has claimed Antioch with the weapons and the bodies of their own dead, perhaps he has also died.

He would have crawled on his belly in the sand until he scrubbed his skin raw, for the sake of Jerusalem; if only he had not promised his body to God as well, and been used thereby!

How else has he arrived here inside of Antioch, other than resurrection out of season?

***

He fights off blind panic by talking to God, whether or not God is listening, which He really should be, considering that this army – that *each iteration* of this army – has been arrayed for His Glory and His Heavenly City. He paces the walls of the citadel, making himself a perfect target for arrows. There are no arrows in this century. Arrows would be too easy.

Thomas, who has never been God, takes his hand by the wrist and makes him sit still. Michel sinks down next to him and leans on his shoulder. Thomas hates when he does that, and has said so. Thomas hates it, and this time he brings his hand up to pat Michel's hair gingerly, so Michel throws every sort of caution to the wind: if Thomas is being kind to him, he must be being exceptionally pathetic this time around. Perhaps pathos will get him closer.

"The Jerusalem we could get," he says, "the conquerable one, the one that's full of people, the one that's got buses that get suicide-bombed and Hebrew University and the Dome of the Rock, that one's all so much impossible dross." He spits the words. *Dross.* Like dust, it clings to his lips.

"Have you earned the heavenly one?" Thomas asks him.

Michel will receive the heavenly Jerusalem when he finally succumbs to famine and the perfect entrapment of this citadel and his siege of it, which is to say *never* – but what he says is, "Would I be here if I had? That's a stupid question, Thomas."

Thomas shrugs, his shoulder moving against Michel's cheek. "I'm here. I keep being here."

"If you're trying to tell me that you've managed to cast off this earthly prison –"

"Absolved I'm *not*," Thomas says.

Michel mutters, "Good."

"Our hands," Thomas says, "when we were here at the beginning, our hands were covered with the blood of this city and every city we ever passed through and devoured, in Thrace and Dacia and Anatolia –"

"Predation, deprivation," Michel says with false brightness.

"Betrayals and deceits," Thomas corrects him, "but in the service of the Lord, and I thought – *why not?* Maybe we'd get to Jerusalem and it would be Heaven after all."

"We found the Holy Lance here," says Michel. "Didn't we? Bartholomew dug it up from a ditch behind the nave in the Cathedral of St. Peter, he was just a monk, I remember – he dug in the dirt until his fingers bled and he was in rags and they might as well have been cloth-of-gold –"

"You dreamed that."

"We *all* dreamed that."

"And we marched out against the Turk the next day and it didn't matter if we lived or died, is that the story you want to tell?" Thomas stares at the paved stone of the citadel wall between his feet. His shoes are wingtip oxfords and not scuffed enough for the walking they've done.

"It didn't matter because we were already dead," Michel says. "And already risen."

"In the forgiving heart of God."

Michel holds his hands out, turns them palm-up, palm-down. They are grey, wizened, windblasted and decaying. "Right here and right now."

Thomas stands up, so fast that he leaves Michel listing violently sideways. He refuses to look at Michel in his true bodily state; instead he stares at the sky as if it was actually Heaven.

"This is wrong," Michel says. His tongue is a desiccated slug of muscle, dry and drying in his mouth. The skin across his cheeks cracks with the effort, and the desert air pours through the stringy shards of what remains. "Maybe we should have come by ocean –"

Thomas interrupts him. "That is a *worse* story," he says, too fast, stumbling over the words. "In that one, we glut ourselves on silver marks and set the Library of Constantinople on fire and desecrate – everything, Michel –" He stops talking. In the silence afterward, Michel thinks they both have stopped breathing, the fiction of the necessity of air at last exposed as a pretense.

It is a long time before Michel can find the will within himself to ask, abject, "What am I supposed to do differently?"

Slowly, Thomas turns to face him. "Why do you think I know?" he asks. He has become transparent. The sand on the wind blows through him, strikes Michel's face.

* * *

Rain is falling into the Bosporus, harder, a rush of pattering sound. Michel opens his eyes. The dust pours from his mouth as if it is chrism and *he* is the reliquary. He blinks, and blinks, and finds Thomas, kneeling at the side of the bed.

"How does one," Michel says, his voice crackling, "stop from wanting Heaven."

Thomas is gathering the dust in printless fingers, making a pile of it on the sheet. He looks up at Michel, and Michel thinks the cast of his mouth is hopeful. He can't be sure. Hopeful is not one of Thomas's standard expressions.

Thomas says, "Patience."

He will make a charm of the desert-dust, a sympathetic compass.

Michel imagines it around his neck in a philter, and shudders. "That is not enough. Desire also is patient."

"Perhaps so is God."

"Then there would be some reachable equality. I dreamed all of the dead –" He stands. He goes to the window, opens it, shoves his hands – whole, unmarked flesh – through the narrow gap. The rain on his palms smells of nothing but water.

"And this is the center of the world. You are not cast out so very far, Michel."

He makes a cup of his hands, allows the rain to pool in it.

When he turns around Thomas is waiting for him, standing at his shoulder and holding out his coat over one arm. His face remains in that hesitant, unsettled state that Michel doesn't have a name for.

"We ought to go," he says.

Michel thinks of the road, stretching endless before them; the mirage of the holy city, ephemeral in the desert. "Better question, Thomas. Will we stop?"

"Which recension of us do you want to tell?"

Michel tips his cupped hands over and lets what he had gathered fall in indistinguishable rivulets onto the carpet. Emptied, the vessel of his palms feels transmuted, slick without water.

Thomas encloses his palms in his own, as if he is grateful, and smiles.

Thank You To Our Supporters

Many thanks to our patrons and supporters, especially:

Sarah Naomi Scott

Natalie Weizenbaum

Emily Anderson • Shelly Jones

Martin Cohen • Fen • Tessa N

J'nae Rae Spano • Tory Hoke

S. Kay Nash • Kayla

Maria Haskins • Jen G

Suzanne Thackston • GriffinFire

Want to see your name here? Become a patron!
patreon.com/lunastation

About the Cover Artist

Kirbi Fagan is a Metro Detroit based illustrator who specializes in creating art for book covers and comics. Her illustrations are known for their magical themes, nostalgic mood and feminine heroines. She received her bachelor's degree in Illustration from Kendall College of Art and Design.

Kirbi is passionate about participating in the illustration community both online and at large. Currently, she teaches illustration at College for Creative Studies in Downtown Detroit. When not painting, Kirbi enjoys writing stories, spending time with her family and rollerblading with her dogs, Sophie and Maisey.

You can find more of her work at:

www.kirbifagan.com

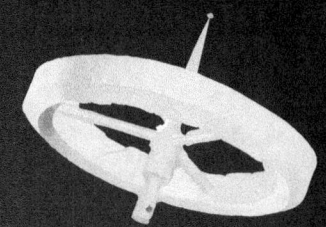

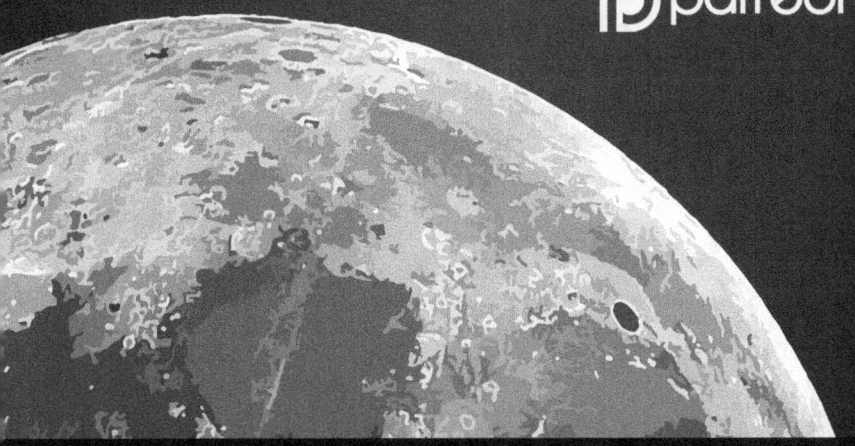